Gift Aid

20   70780305   5822

The Ghost of Edinburgh

Gerard Francis Quinn

Author's note

Some of the establishments mentioned in this publication such as Sandy Bell's and The Hebrides are real places. Others such as The Irish Club, The Grey Mare, The Minerva Hotel and Il Pescatore Restaurant are purely fictitious.
All characters are fictitious and any resemblance to real persons, living or dead is purely coincidental.

ISBN: 9798693251038

Thy sons, Edina, social, kind
With open arms, the stranger hail;
Their views enlarged, their lib'ral mind
Above the narrow rural vale.

Robert Burns
Address to Edinburgh 1786

Contents

Chapter 1

Leo Coyne left the Coventry Irish Club, fiddle case in hand and headed down the street. He'd been to the weekly fiddle class, run by the Comhaltas Group, and had had a few tunes and a few pints afterwards. He liked to walk as much as he could both to keep fit and save money. It was eleven thirty at night and the walk home would take him about half an hour. He turned around the corner and saw a group of five lads approaching. He nonchalantly crossed the road in a diagonal line as if walking towards one of the parked cars.

Trouble was they also crossed the road.

'Got a machine gun in that case mate?' said the tallest one.

Leo winked 'Can't be too careful these days.'

'Not funny,' said another 'Let's roll him.'

Leo tensed. Five of them, he'd got no chance.

'I've got nothing lads. I don't want any trouble.'

Leo kept walking. He felt a kick at the back of his legs.

'Leave him, Baz,' said the tall one.

'Let's have him,' said Baz.

'I said leave him!'

Leo kept walking.

They didn't seem to be following but he daren't look back.

He increased his pace but did not run.

He walked for a further ten minutes or so and knew he would soon be at the main road where there would be people and traffic about.

Just then a figure emerged from an adjoining street. About five –ten, striped trackie bottoms and black hoodie … it was Baz.

He stepped in front of Leo.

'Thought you'd got away, you fiddle playing wufter,' he snarled at Leo.

'Listen, this violin brings pleasure to a lot of people, I call it the peacemaker,' Leo tried to keep him talking.

'Don't give me any bullshit!'

'I want your phone, your watch and your money, now!'

Leo saw Baz's hand go inside his jacket; he just got a glimpse of the handle of the knife as he smashed him full in the face with the hard fiddle case.

Baz staggered backwards. Leo smashed him again with the case just for good measure and Baz fell to the ground.

Now Leo was running.

He reached the main road, turned the corner, and stopped to get his breath. He saw a black cab approaching and stuck his thumb out.

A squeal of brakes and one of Coventry's own was beside him.

He jumped in and directed the driver.

Leo was panting, and the cabbie noticed. 'In some kind of trouble, matey?' the cabbie asked.

'No, I've just had a race with a pal … a bit of boozy daftness.'

The taxi pulled up outside Leo's flat and Leo pushed a note through the aperture.

'Keep the change, mate.'

'Thanks,' said the cabbie, eyeing him suspiciously.

Leo watched the cab drive off, looked around and then stepped in and climbed the stairs to his first-floor flat. He unlocked the two locks on his sturdy front door, entered, put the lights on and tapped in the alarm code. He went through to the kitchen and looked at the fiddle case. It seemed clean enough, but he wiped it over anyway. Peacemaker indeed, he thought to himself.

He didn't usually drink at home but was still trembling. He sloshed a good measure of his favourite malt, Ardbeg, into a tumbler and poured a large glass of water. He took them through to his lounge and put them on the little table by his armchair.

He sat down, took a sip of the whiskey, swirled it around in his mouth and washed it down with some of the water.

He thought about putting some music on but decided it was a bit late and it might annoy the neighbours. Besides, he needed to think. He rolled himself a cigarette, lit it, took a drag, had another sip of Ardbeg, and started to feel a bit better.

He thought about the events of the evening, he wasn't proud of himself. He hated violence; he'd seen enough of it in his childhood and youth and was determined to break the chain.

Things were getting worse in the area but since his redundancy and divorce, he was thinking of moving away anyway, there was nothing to keep him there really. What would he miss? Well, he'd miss Pat and Mary, Sheedy, Fergus, and the rest of the crowd at the club, but that was about it really.

He thought about moving to Ireland where his parents came from, but something was stopping him.

He poured some more whiskey. He stared at the bottle. Ardbeg . . . he'd first tasted the Islay malt on one of his visits to Edinburgh. Edinburgh! He thought. That's it, that's where I need to be right now.

Chapter 2

The next morning Leo called in at the Express Mini Supermarket on his way to the station. He grabbed two packs of sandwiches, a packet of crisps, a bottle of water, and a couple of newspapers. He paid for them and stuffed them into the last bit of space in his rucksack.

He boarded the 9:11 to Birmingham New Street, which would leave him plenty of time to catch the 10:20 Edinburgh train.

As the train left Coventry behind, he thought about his childhood, growing up on the Wood End housing estate. The place had become a nightmare. Ha! 'The Live and Let Live' pub became known as 'The Live and Let Die'. Of course, it was gone now – a health centre built in its place. But the estate wasn't always like that. Leo's dad and most of his mates' dads went off to work (mostly on pushbikes) in one of the many motor manufacturing factories and came home on a Friday with a brown wage packet, treats for the moms and 'Lucky Bags' for the kids. They kept their gardens neat, trimmed the hedges and grew vegetables in the back. All this changed in the 1980's when the jobs disappeared, and society changed for ever.

Many of Leo's mates had ended up in prison and some of them had ended up dead, but Leo had managed to drag himself out of it. He got himself an apprenticeship and worked his way up in the company. He learnt to play the fiddle and would play in pub sessions or at the Irish club in the evenings and could also sing a few songs. At weekends or holidays, he'd escape to the Lake District, the Yorkshire Dales or Ireland where he could combine his interests in fell walking and music. He eventually got married and bought a semi on the edge of the city but that was then...

The train braked and jerked Leo out of his reverie, it came to a halt outside of New Street. There must have been another train ahead of it. It waited a few minutes and then trundled into the station. Leo stood up and grabbed his fiddle case and rucksack from the luggage rack. He left the train and found the platform for his connection. 'Edinburgh 10:20 On time,' read the sign.

He'd booked online, a double room at the Minerva Hotel in Cowgate; a single wasn't much cheaper, and he liked a double bed. Also, you usually got shoved in a pokey room at the back of the top floor if you booked a single.

He also booked his train reservation online. He looked at the printout: Coach B Seat 19, it read.

The train pulled in. It was a Pendolino and he found his way to his seat. I'm in luck, he thought, a table seat, forward facing and next to a window. He liked to be able to view certain parts of the country as he passed through familiar or favourite areas. He removed his newspapers from his rucksack and squeezed it and his fiddle case into the luggage space above his seat.

He watched the Black Country towns of Oldbury, Dudley, Tipton and Coseley flash by. All these places had their Wood Ends, large urban sprawls where, in his opinion, the working class had been turned into the criminal class, but so did Edinburgh, he supposed. Still, he was only going there to suss it out and sort himself out.

The train stopped at Wolverhampton, people got off and on. A couple sat down opposite him, but no one sat in the unreserved seat next to him. Even better, there were no screaming kids. He usually attracted them like a magnet!

He settled down to read his newspapers, The *i*, which he thought was fairly unbiased and actually acknowledged that Scotland existed, and the Mirror, which he thought had gone downhill a bit, but he liked doing the quiz word.

The journey passed quietly until the train reached Preston, where a tired and harassed looking woman with a crying baby daughter got on and headed unerringly down the aisle to the seat next to Leo. She sat down, baby on lap and gave Leo an apologetic smile which he returned.

The little girl was crying quite loudly. Ah well, thought Leo, at least half the journey was peaceful. The woman tried her best to calm the baby and Leo concentrated on his crossword.

Leo was lost in his thoughts until he became aware that it was now quiet, he glanced sideways to see that they were both fast asleep.

Lancaster and Oxenholme came and went, and Leo was admiring the beautiful Lune valley. The Howgill fells came into view and he remembered walking these fells in a day some years ago. The train tilted into a curve in the line and the mother and daughter, still asleep, fell on to Leo's shoulder. He hadn't bothered to put the armrest down when the seat was unoccupied and now he was frightened to move for fear of waking them. Leo took a deep breath, relaxed and closed his eyes. It felt strangely comforting and he drifted off to sleep himself.

The train slowed down and Leo opened his eyes. He recognised the outskirts of Carlisle and decided to wake his sleeping companions. He gently eased them sideways and the woman woke up.

'Oh! I'm sorry, I'm so sorry,' she said.

'It's quite all right, it was peaceful, but I wondered where you were getting off,' Leo replied.

'Carlisle,' she said.

'We're just coming into Carlisle now,' Leo informed her.

The little girl started crying as they got up to leave the train.

'I really am sorry,' the mother apologised again.

'Don't you worry about it and have a safe onward journey,' Leo replied. He was feeling hungry and took the opportunity to get his rucksack down.

The train continued and was soon taking the big curve through Carstairs, but it didn't stop. This station brought back memories to Leo. When he was a child his mother would take him to stay with her sister in Glasgow, to get away from his father for a few days. The train used to split here and there would be empty seats in the rear of the train which was going to Edinburgh but none in the front section. His mother would drag him along the platform to get in the front section to stand for the rest of the journey to Glasgow.

The train finally reached Edinburgh and Leo left Waverley station through the back entrance. He stood in the street and breathed in the crisp, clear spring air. 'Auld Reekie' no more, he thought. After the long journey, he was tempted to go straight to The Hebrides, which was just up the street to the right, for a pint but thought better of it. He'd done that before, got involved in a music session and it was midnight before he checked into his hotel. Instead he turned left and headed down towards Cowgate.

*****

Fiona Frielle let her assistant, Marie, out of the upmarket perfumery in the New Town and locked the glass door. She picked up the remote control and sent down the window grille from inside the shop. It still allowed the window display to be seen from the street and a classy establishment like this didn't want its appearance spoilt by ugly shutters. She had already locked the safe and the cellar while Marie was still there and was ready to go. She left through the back, locked up and went out into the little yard where her Jaguar XK was parked. She jumped in and threw her coat on the passenger seat. She pressed the remote that opened the gate and drove out into the street. She paused a while to make sure the gate had closed and then drove the short journey to her luxury apartment overlooking the Meadows. These apartments were called tenements, but they were beautiful, elegant old buildings, built of pink sandstone in the Scottish Baronial style with huge rooms, large bay windows and high decorated ceilings. The only disadvantage was there was no lift. Fiona climbed the stairs to her door, went in and hung her coat up. She kicked off her shoes, then took off her smart waistcoat, skirt and blouse and carefully put them on hangers. She put on a huge XXL men's tee-shirt and let her hair down — that's better, she thought — she hated dressing up for her job. She fixed herself a glass of wine, crashed on to the sofa and lit a cigarette. She considered trying the new gourmet food delivery service, well, she could afford it, she told herself. She'd got it all, well paid job, flash car and luxury apartment, all paid for by Jake.

When Fiona first saw Jake McCullen, standing six feet four, long golden locks and flashy clothes, she thought he was a rock star. Fresh faced and impressionable, she was amazed when he took an interest in her. Against her family's wishes she'd come over from Donegal to Edinburgh to study at university. Her family were small time farmers and they wanted her to marry Edward Boyle, the son of a wealthy local landowner, who had taken a fancy to her. Whenever there was a social occasion Edward was invited and it was developing into an arranged marriage situation, but Fiona was having none of it. She was out of there, much to the displeasure of her parents and presumably Edward.

She'd taken up with Jake and things were fantastic to start with — a whirlwind of top restaurants, nightclubs and parties — but that was then and now she was just one of Jake's girls.

Jake had set her up at the perfumery; at least he hadn't put her on the game. It was just one of

Jake's many money laundering outlets for his drug, extortion and people trafficking empire. He owned many legitimate businesses and they were all top end. He also knew the right people all the way to the top of Edinburgh society - he was untouchable.

So yes, she'd got it all, but she knew in her heart it was all worthless really, but there was one thing she liked about Edinburgh ...

*****

Deep in the bowels of the Old Town, Leo emerged from his hotel and headed down the dark cobbled street. Once home to the gentry, Cowgate became a poor overcrowded slum area and was known as 'Little Ireland' due to the large numbers of Irish immigrants that lived here. Indeed, the famous Irish republican socialist, James Connolly, was born here. Now an area of bars and nightclubs it still has an intimidating aura, hemmed in, as it is by tall, dark tenements.

Refreshed by a nap and a shower Leo was ready for a pint. He'd got the fiddle with him and decided he might get an early tune at the 'Heb'. He stopped at a corner pub and looked at the menu in the window.

Reasonable, he thought.

He looked beyond the menu into the pub. People were eating and the food on their plates looked good.

He looked beyond the people who were eating and spotted four real ale hand pumps along the bar.

It's getting better, he thought.

He made a mental note of it for later and carried on.

He came upon the rather shabby looking Grey Mare and contemplated it. He'd spotted it before and was intrigued. It looked like what some people might call a bit of a dive, but you can't really tell from the outside. Anyway, you often meet the most interesting characters in these sorts of places.

He decided to go in.

The bar was empty except for two men and the barman at the end of the bar, all with their heads in the racing pages.

All three looked up at him and quickly looked away.

Eventually the barman grudgingly trudged over to him.

'An' whit can Ah dae fur ye?'

Leo eyed the Guinness pump, its cream background turned orange with age.

'A pint of Guinness, please.'

'Ye ken we huvnae sauld Guinness in haur since nineteen-seventy-six —'

How was I to know? Leo thought to himself.

'—It's Eckie or naethin.'

'Eckie it is then,' replied Leo, wondering what 'Eckie' was.

He watched the barman pour a pint of McEwen's Export and bring it to him. He gave him a fiver and the barman brought back the change.

'Thank you,' said Leo.

'An thenk ye,' said the barman with a puzzled look on his face.

Leo stayed where he was on a stool at the bar with his fiddle case at his feet. He watched the barman return to the other end of the bar to the two men and the racing paper. They whispered among themselves, glanced down at Leo and like before, quickly looked away.

Leo took a sip of the fizzy liquid (he preferred real ale) and looked around the bar. It was pure 1960's or no, 1950's even.

The bar top was green mottled Formica with a plastic gold trim that had somehow stood the test of time. On the wall there were scrolls and pictures of Spanish ladies adorned with fruit. A giant sombrero hung from a light fitting and various souvenirs of Torremolinos were randomly displayed around the room. A bench seat ran along one wall with small rectangular tables and steel framed chairs. On the tables were sauce bottles and menus of the sausage and chips variety.

Leo took another drink from his glass and suddenly the peace was shattered as a large and noisy family group entered the pub; kids in buggies, older kids in football shirts, parents with shopping, auntie, uncle, granny, and a dog. Leo decided it was time to go. He rolled a cigarette and drained his pint, picked up his fiddle case and headed for the door without looking back. He stood in the doorway and lit his cigarette. Time for the Heb, he thought. He set off down the street and eventually emerged in the High Street part of the Royal Mile. He vaguely recollected that somewhere around here there were steps down past two small pubs that came out opposite Waverley and not far from the Heb. He saw a large archway marked Carrubber's Close and thought, ah this must be it. He went through it and started down the steps.

He soon realised they were not the steps he had in mind. They were dark and dank, and nobody seemed to be using them. He carried on anyway, assuming they must lead roughly to where he wanted to go.

He thought he saw something move in the shadows below.

He dropped his cigarette, stood on it, and carried on down.

As he came to the level part two baseball-capped figures emerged from behind a buttress on the left and barred his way.

'Got any cigarettes, Pal?' A gruff voice spoke.

'I've only got roll-ups,' Leo replied.

'That's all right, your money will do.'

Leo felt the adrenalin rush.

He started spinning, round and round, like a demented whirling dervish, his fiddle case at the end of his outstretched arm. Round and round, he could smell urine and saw fleeting images of graffiti on the walls, needles on the ground, ventilation grilles, twisted drainpipes and the whites of their startled eyes, there was mad music playing in his head as he smacked one of them with the end of his fiddle case and next time round, crack! He caught the other.

Leo took off down the sloping close and soon found himself in the street below. He turned left under a bridge and past a sentry of wheelie bins. He saw the railway buildings and realised where he was. He kept on going until he came to the station entrance, he looked to his left where steps led up and a sign on the wall read 'Fleshmarket Close'. Damn! He thought, that's where I meant to have come down. He stopped outside the Doric pub to get his breath and looked back down the street.

No sign of them. He took a deep breath and went next door into the Hebrides.

He didn't really feel like playing now and tried to conceal his fiddle by holding it straight down by the side of his leg and looked people straight in the eye as he walked to the bar. The peacemaker strikes again, he thought, as he slid it down between his feet and the base of the bar counter.

He sat on a bar stool and ordered a pint of Guinness. No problems this time, as the cheery Eastern European barmaid three quarter-filled a glass, took his money, and registered it in the till, whereupon an electronic sign above the bar displayed what he was drinking and its price for all to see. She returned with his full pint.

'There you are.'

'Perfect,' said Leo.

'You are welcome,' she replied.

Leo liked the Heb. It was a meeting place for people down from the Highlands and Islands and also exiles, a bit too *Teuchterish* for some Edinburgh natives perhaps, but a real pub with a lively atmosphere. There was a smallish fellow behind a huge piano accordion knocking out what Leo called Scottish Top Ten: *Marie's Wedding, Skye Boat Song, Mingulay Boat Song, Scotland the Brave* and the like. A large relief map of the actual islands ran the length of the wall behind him.

From his position at the bar, Leo had a good view out on to the street through the large Celtic patterned window and was keeping one eye on it. He noticed two darkly dressed figures in baseball caps approaching. It's gotta be them, he thought and leaving his half-finished pint on the bar, he headed down to the toilets. He lingered awhile in case they were checking the place out and then thought what if they come down here? He decided to go back up. The accordionist was playing a rousing version of the *Jig of Slurs* — it was battle music, as he climbed the steps. He entered the bar and looked around. There was no sign of them so he re-joined his pint at the bar, checking the window as he sat down. A succession of black cabs was going past, plying their trade at Waverley station. He decided it would be wise to move on so finished his pint and left.

He stood in the doorway and looked up and down the street. It was quite busy with people coming and going. Leo hailed a cab. Just then he heard a shout 'There's the bastard!'

He saw the two youths running up the street.

He jumped into the cab.

'Sandy Bell's please and don't let those two in.'

The cab pulled away as one of them made a grab for the door handle, the other kicked the back of the cab.

When the driver was clear of them, he said, 'Shall I get the polis?'

'No, better not thanks, they'd probably charge me with assault.'

Leo explained what had happened in Carrubber's Close.

'Fair enough,' said the cabbie, doubtfully.

He drove on and took a circuitous route dropping Leo right outside the door of Sandy Bell's.

At the bar, Leo scanned the hand pumps and spotted one of his favourite beers.

'A pint of Bitter and Twisted please,' Leo ordered.

While the barman was pulling it, Leo studied the large collection of mainly Speyside malts and then spotted the unmistakeable dark green bottle hiding behind the others.

'... and a single Ardbeg as well, please.'

'Good choice,' said the barman.

The barman placed Leo's drinks on the bar.

Leo said, 'Have one yourself,' as he handed him a note.

'Cheers,' said the barman.

He returned with his change and beckoned Leo closer.

'A mucker ay mine phoned me up the-day frae hospital, he said yoo've got tae gie me it ay haur, aw they ur feedin' me oan is tatties, neeps an' whisky!' Ah said, 'what ward ur ye oan?' He said, 'the burns unit!'

Leo struggled to understand his accent but got it just in time, 'Ha ha, good one,' he laughed. It pays to keep in with the bar staff and here you get a joke for good measure.

The fiddles and the flutes were playing at the far end of the bar as Leo took a sip from his pint. He was still shaking from his earlier experiences as he contemplated his dram. He took a sip of the smoky, peaty liquid. Ah! That's better, he thought and began to relax when, suddenly, he felt a slap across his back. He almost jumped out of his skin.

'Leo, you're back!' It was Dewar.

He shook Leo's hand enthusiastically. 'Ye'v yer fiddle wid ye? Aye,' Dewar answered his own question. 'Will ye be joining us?'

'That would be an honour and a pleasure,' Leo replied.

Leo had met Dewar on previous trips to Edinburgh and had played with him before. He was a tough, craggy faced, no nonsense sort of bloke who didn't suffer fools easily, a guitarist and singer in his own right but on accompanist duty tonight.

Leo knocked back his dram, took his pint and his fiddle over and joined the group. He grabbed a spare stool and eased in on the periphery of the session. He took out his bow and decided to rosin it as he hadn't done it for about a week. He then took up his fiddle, tuned it to the others and joined in quietly with the tunes he knew. He got a few nods of approval and other signs in the unspoken language that musicians have.

'Gie us a tune then Leo,' said Dewar when a set finished, and it went quiet.

Leo launched into a set of reels, *Maudabawn Chapel, The Wild Irishman* and *The Moher*, a set he knew they would all know and could help him out if he faltered.

'A bit shaky arenae ye?' said Dewar when it came to the end.

'Always nervous in such illustrious company,' Leo replied.

'Och c'maun!' Dewar scoffed.

Leo explained about his earlier experiences in Carrubber's Close and outside the Hebrides.

Dewar laughed as if it was nothing. 'Make sure ye gang doon Fleshmarket next time and if there's ony muggers ye can nip in th' Halfway Hoose.'

The session continued, and musicians came and went, disappearing outside, presumably for a smoke and a bit of blether and reappearing five or ten minutes later. Dewar disappeared and returned with a couple of pints. He placed the paler one in front of Leo.

'There ye go, Bitter and Twisted, just like yourself!'

'Cheers, you're probably right,' replied Leo.

'Have ye been in the Captain's?' Dewar enquired.

'In where?'

'The Captain's bar, you'd like it, great for music and a great pub.'

'Where is it?'

'Ye ken th' Oak?'

'Yes.'

'Come oot o' thaur an' cross the road, heed oot o' town alang South Bridge an it's next oan the reit, South College Street, ye canna muss it.'

'Thanks, I'll have to give it a try.'

The session continued.

A piper took out his pipes and started tuning them. At that Dewar headed for the bar, pint in hand and stayed there chatting to a few of his mates. Once the piper was satisfied with his tuning, he blasted out various tunes accompanied by a solitary bodhran player. Eventually the bell for last orders rang; Leo decided he'd better get Dewar a drink and went up to the bar.

'Dewar, what are you having?'

'Don't get any more, we're going tae Whistle Binkies...there's a guid band on the night.'

'But it's half past twelve!'

'That's ok, it's open till three, are ye comin' wi' us?'

Leo thought about it for a few seconds, 'Ok, count me in.'

'Good man!' Dewar replied, 'You can get the drinks in there.'

So, Leo found himself heading back in the direction of his earlier altercations, to Whistle Binkies with Dewar and his merry band.

Chapter 3

Leo woke with a start; he was in his hotel bed but could not remember getting back. He looked at his watch, it was nine o'clock. He felt a bit rough but the main thing he felt was hunger. It dawned on him that the last time he had eaten was on the train the day before. He quickly showered and went down for breakfast, grabbing a free newspaper on the way. The breakfast bar was self-service, so Leo piled it high and ate hungrily. After several cups of coffee, he began to feel a bit better and decided that, rather than going back to bed, a good walk would do him good.

He made his way down to Holyrood. It was a bright, clear spring day and this and the prospect of some fantastic views made him decide to climb Arthur's Seat. After a steep climb he soon attained the summit and indeed the views made the climb worthwhile. A 360-degree vista from the Pentland Hills to the south, all across the city and north to the Firth of Forth, Leith and Portobello with the Hibees' ground, Easter Road, seemingly almost within touching distance.

Leo decided to explore further and headed east, down past a small loch where he crossed a road and eventually came to a muddy track at the edge of the park. He followed this and came to a flight of steps which he counted as he descended. As he reached 199, he emerged into the wonderful village within a city, Duddingston. With its loch, ancient kirk and cottages and its rural aspect, it was hard to believe this was still Edinburgh. Better still, here he found Scotland's oldest pub, so the sign informed him, The Sheep Heid. Leo just had to go in.

It didn't disappoint; a beautiful panelled interior and his favourite ales on tap. He ordered a Harvistoun and took it out into the courtyard. He sat at a table and rolled a cigarette. The events of the previous day ran through his mind. He remembered Dewar telling him about the Captain's Bar and decided to give it a try that evening. He was drifting away when a shadow cast over him. The sun had gone behind the roof of the building, so he decided to move back into the sunshine.   As he stood up a rather distinguished looking gentleman beckoned him over 'These seats are more comfortable'.

Leo joined him. The only difference was that the wrought iron seats had cushions fitted.

'Beautiful day,' his new companion remarked. 'Been for a walk?'

'Yes,' Leo replied, 'Arthur's Seat, to work up a thirst.'

'On holiday?'

'Sort of, but flat hunting as well, my name's Leo by the way.'

'James,' he offered his hand. 'Where are you from?'

'Near Birmingham,' Leo replied.

'And you want to live in Edinburgh … why?'

'I just like it.'

'Are you staying in the city?'

'Yes, hotel, Old Town.'

'You could walk back along the Innocent Railway,' James informed him.

'Innocent Railway?' Leo looked puzzled.

'Yes … it's a cycle route now, takes you right into the city.'

'But why's it called the Innocent Railway?'

'Well,' James began to explain, 'the mythology is that it's called that because no-one was ever killed building it or using it, but the reality is that it was horse drawn well into the days of steam and many people were afraid of steam engines. The writer, Dr Robert Chalmers wrote: "in the very contemplation of the innocence of the railway you find your heart rejoiced" and thus its name was coined.'

'You're very knowledgeable, what do you do?' Leo asked.

'I work at the university,' James replied without elaborating further.

Leo drained the last of his pint. 'Better not have any more.'

'So how do you get to this Innocent Railway?' Leo asked.

'Turn right outside the door and right at the end of the street, carry on along the main road, you'll see where it crosses the road.'

'Thanks,' said Leo, 'it's been interesting talking to you, bye now.'

Leo got up to leave.

'The Jazz Bar's my local if you're in town,' James called out after him.

*****

It was early evening as Sean Consadigne set out from his tiny flat in the Dumbiedykes and headed into town. He didn't drink much these days but liked an early evening pint. The shame of being seen by his family handcuffed to two prison officers at his own father's funeral made him vow to mend his ways when he was released. He'd got mixed up in the drugs world and took the rap for a much bigger fish. Because of that they'd left him alone after he came out. He knew these people, but he kept out of it. Didn't do drugs and even packed in smoking. The one indulgence in his now quiet life was a few early evening pints. He was making his way to his regular haunt: the Scotsman's Lounge, and his route took him past the Grey Mare. He hadn't been in the Mare for a long time and didn't particularly like it, but something made him stop and decide to go in.

'Hello, Sean isn't it?' said the barman.

'Aye,' Sean replied and ordered.

He recognised the three characters at the corner of the bar and although he didn't know them too well, he knew their names.

'Hi Tam, hi John, hi Archie.' He spoke to them and they all nodded in reply.

The barman passed Sean his drink and continued 'Your brother was in yesterday, still asking for Guinness, we hadn't seen him for over a year.'

Sean contemplated the barman, whose lined face told that he'd probably seen and heard it all in his lifetime, but whose pale blue eyes seemed kindly.

'My brother's been dead for over a year!' said Sean, grimly.

The barman looked at him incredulously but could see that he was serious. 'I'm sorry to hear that but he must have a double, even had a fiddle with him.'

'It might have been his ghost,' piped up Archie, a smallish fellow with a red face and mischievous grin.

'Och ye dinna believe in ony o' tha' nonsense do ye?' said John, the serious one amongst them.

'It isnae nonsense Johnny boy, Embre's world famous for ghosts, why, even this pub is named after a ghost!'

'What, the Grey Mare?' said Tam, a man who was always ready to take the mick.

'Aye, the story goes that a captain in seventeenth century clothing, mounted on a grey mare, gallops towards the pub, ye can hear the hooves on the sets, he stops ootside and then just disappears but … it is said, every time he visits someone dies!'

Sean gulped his drink; the anger was rising in him.

'It's a guid story,' said Tam 'and I've heard Blair Street Vaults is full of ghosts.'

'Aye it is and don't even mention The Banshee Labyrinth.'

'Why not?' said John.

'The ghost of Rosie, a prostitute, scratches and bites male staff and customers,' said Archie, becoming animated.

'Are ye sure it's not one of your ex-girlfriends?' said Tam.

They all laughed except Sean.

'These stories are all very well Archie but ye canna prove them, I mean have you ever seen a ghost?' John asked.

Archie was silent.

'Well have you? Come on, out with it man, have you?'

'Well no but …'

'No but what?' John wasn't letting him off the hook.

'But I've felt one!' exclaimed Archie.

'Felt one! Felt one! Where, when?'

'Same place as I was just telling you about, The Banshee and the ghost is called … Six Finger Bill!'

They all started to laugh but Sean didn't seem too amused.

'Och c'maun Archie,' John said, when he'd stopped laughing.

'Sit down Johnny boy and I'll tell ye mair,' Archie gestured towards the bench seat and they sat down opposite one and other at the table.

'I was in there for a late one on the way hame one night, must have been about two in the morning. I was sat at a table just like this and one by one all the customers left. Usually there was a late influx when the other places closed but that night there was just me and the barman left.' Archie dropped his one arm slowly under the table. 'I was just finishing my drink when …'

Archie grabbed John's ankle and John let out a shriek: 'Aagh!'

'… Six Finger Bill grabbed my ankle just like that.'

They all fell about laughing but Sean drained his glass and banged it on the bar.

'I've had enough of this, Kevin's only been dead a year and you lot seem to think it's a big joke.'

'They don't mean it like that,' said the barman.

But Sean was not to be placated.

'I'm outa here, you disrespectful parcel o' bastards,' and with a slam of the door he was gone.

*****

Leo Coyne removed the *Do Not Disturb* sign from the hotel room door. He was in the habit of having an afternoon nap and now set out into the early evening refreshed by both the nap and a hearty meal at the place he'd discovered the previous evening, the World's End. His journey back along the Innocent Railway that afternoon had been pleasant and incident free, although he had entered the 517 metres long tunnel with some foreboding. He needn't have worried, the only danger being a couple of cyclists, whose tunnel amplified bells nearly caused him a heart failure. Emerging in the St Leonard's area of the city, the contrast from rural to urban was as striking as the brightness that dazzled his eyes. This evening he'd decided to go to the Captain's Bar and had his fiddle with him but wanted to try a couple of other places first. He was walking up the steeply inclined Blair Street, with its sombre grey buildings, when a woman coming down on the other side of the street stopped dead in her tracks and stared at him. He looked across at her, but she looked away and quickly moved on. This was disconcerting as he'd experienced a couple of similar situations since he'd been in Edinburgh. He carried on and after a little while he looked over his shoulder.

She'd crossed the road and was following him! He stopped and turned around. She disappeared into a doorway. Leo shrugged and carried on across the Royal Mile to the Scotsman's Lounge, looked behind him again and went in. This was a proper pub, used by locals although slap bang in the middle of tourist territory. He ordered a half of Guinness and settled down to listen to the early evening guitarist who sang amusing versions of standard folk ballads. There was a Scottish version of Simon and Garfunkel's *The Boxer* and even a *Teuchter frae Skye* version of *Ghost Riders in the Sky*.

Leo rolled a cigarette and went for a smoke, standing by an A-board outside the pub.

'Excuse me; are you doing the ghost tours?' A lady with an American accent asked him.

'What?' replied a startled Leo.

'The ghost tours.' She pointed at the A-board which read:

'Queue here for next *EDINBURGH GHOST TOUR*'

Leo laughed, 'Oh, I see what you mean. Sorry no, I've just come out for a smoke.'

He finished his cigarette, went back in, finished his drink, and grabbed his fiddle. He left the pub and walked aimlessly along the Royal Mile, turned left into St Giles Street, then down Bank Street, without any particular destination in mind.

*****

Sean Consadigne marched up the street, overtaking the dawdling tourists. Why did I go in there? He asked himself as he made his way from The Grey Mare to his local. He was about to turn into Cockburn Street when he spotted Heather, his sister's friend, who called him over.
'Sean,' she said, 'I've just seen Kevin's double, had a fiddle with him as well, uncanny it was.'
'Where did you see him?' asked Sean.
'I followed him up Blair Street (Sean remembered Tam's words: 'Blair Street Vaults is full of ghosts') and he went into The Scotsman's.
'Is he in there now?' asked Sean.
'No, he came out for a ciggy, he was standing by that A-board.' Heather pointed at it.
Sean read the words: 'Queue here for next *EDINBURGH GHOST TOUR*'
'This is crazy, where did he go?'
'He went back in and came straight back out with his fiddle and came past here and turned into St Giles Street. I stopped following him

because he kept looking back and I wasn't sure what to do.'

'How long ago?' asked Sean.

Just now, a few minutes ago,' Heather replied.

'Thanks Heather, I'll get to the bottom of this,' said Sean as he hurried off in the direction of St Giles Street.

*****

Leo passed the baroque style Bank of Scotland building, and as he neared the bottom of Bank Street, he could hear a cacophony of loud screams and then he saw it… a ghost train. A fun fair had set up along Market Street for the holiday. Leo thought this must be one scary ghost train to cause this much screaming but as he turned the corner, he saw the reason for it, people on a huge pendulum towering about 80 metres above him.

As he craned his neck to look up at it, he heard a voice cry out, 'Roll up! Roll up! For the world's scariest ghost train!'

Leo looked over and to see a burly man by a sign that read 'Help required.'

Curious, he went over to him.

'You have a job vacancy?'

'Yes,' replied the attendant, 'we use real people dressed as ghosts, that's what makes it so scary.'

'That would look good on my CV, used to be a ghost on a ghost train,' said Leo.

The attendant was not impressed. 'It's just a bit of casual for the students really,' he said, sounding slightly irritated.

'Ok, sorry to bother you.'

Leo thought it wise to move on and as The Heb was just down the street decided to go there.

*****

Sean turned into St Giles Street, then strode down Bank Street scanning it from side to side until he came upon the ghost train and the attendant drumming up business.

'Have you seen a guy with a fiddle go past here?' Sean asked him.

'I have,' replied the attendant, 'he was asking about the job.'

The attendant pointed at the sign 'I think he was trying to take the piss, bit of a nutcase if you ask me.'

'Which way'd he go?'

'Down Market Street, through the fair,' the attendant replied.

'Thanks for your help,' said Sean.

Sean crossed the junction at the bottom of Market Street and contemplated The Heb. No, he thought, Kevin never went in there. He cursed himself for thinking he was looking for his dead brother, decided it was ridiculous and headed up Fleshmarket and back to The Scotsman's, but on the way still checked The Halfway House just in case.

Sean sank heavily onto a stool at the Scotsman's and spread his forearms on the bar.

'What's a matter with you?' said the barman, 'you look like you've seen ghost.'

'No, the trouble is I haven't seen a ghost,' replied Sean.

*****

Leo left The Heb after a quiet pint and with the previous night's would-be assailants still in mind, decided to heed Dewar's advice and go up Fleshmarket steps past The Halfway 'Hoose'.

He walked right past The Scotsman's and along the busy South Bridge, then right into South College Street where he contemplated The Captain's Bar. He looked at the array of posters outside advertising music for most nights of the week. There was also a blue plaque commemorating Scotland's infamous poet William McGonagall, who apparently had at one time lived above the establishment. It certainly seems an interesting place, he thought, as he entered the pub.

Leo ordered a pint of Guinness.

'Are you going to play tonight?' the barmaid asked, as she watched him place the fiddle case at his feet.

'I might be if I'm invited,' Leo replied.

'We'd love you to, Liam will make you welcome, come with me and I'll introduce you.'

She emerged from behind the bar.

'What's your name?' She asked him.

'Err, I'm Leo'.

'And you play fiddle?'

'That's right.'

'We always welcome fiddle players here.'

She led him down the long narrow room to an area of two small tables, assorted chairs and walls lined with bookcases. Seated at the far table was a smallish guy with greying hair and a friendly face and on the table an old enamel tin mug with the words 'Tips for musicians' written on it.

'Liam this is Leo, he's come to join in with you,' she said, giving neither of them a choice, 'I'll bring your drink down to you Leo.'

Liam stood up and shaking Leo's hand he said, 'Appearing tonight, Liam and Leo; that sounds good.'

Liam did indeed make Leo welcome and was an absolute gentleman. Leo hit it off with him right away and they quickly developed an understanding with Leo accompanying Liam's songs and Liam backing Leo's fiddle tunes. Even better Liam gave Leo the opportunity to sing a few songs and backed him on guitar. The room was filling up nicely and four girls who looked like students sat opposite them, applauding noisily after each number. A couple of young lads soon joined them, one of whom went over to the musicians and announced that he was Canadian, was studying seafaring songs and could they do *Lord Franklin*?

'I'm not sure of all the words,' said Liam.

'I know it,' said Leo, 'I do it in D,' he said turning to Liam, 'do you know the tune?'

'Aye, give it a go if you like.'

So, Leo obliged.

As Leo was about halfway through the song a tall, rather striking blonde woman came from the bar, glanced at Leo, and sat among the younger girls.

Leo concentrated on the song but whenever he sneaked a look in her direction she seemed to be looking right into his eyes. He forgot the words of a verse so played an instrumental verse on the fiddle while he tried to remember them, but the crowd thought it was intentional and applauded the solo. He finished the song without looking up and the Canadian came over and shook his hand. 'Great version,' he said, 'I'll get you a drink.'

'Thanks,' Leo replied.

'Almost blew it,' Leo whispered to Liam, 'mind you I was distracted.'

'Really?' Liam seemed surprised.

A large red-haired man with a handlebar moustache came over and pulled up a tiny stool that he somehow managed to sit on and started chatting to Liam. For some reason, Leo imagined him to be an Aberdeenshire farmer, but it turned out he was a friend of Liam's from Fife. He then proceeded to give a long and evidently humorous recitation that Leo could understand very little of but laughed along with it anyway. This was followed by a couple of equally indecipherable songs which earned loud applause and cheering and then he was gone back to his presumably more comfortable seat in the depths of the bar.

'He's a stoatin laddie!' said Liam.

'He certainly is,' replied Leo, hoping he was saying the right thing.

'Play us a couple o' reels Leo, let's keep it lively.'

So, Leo embarked on a set of reels that he knew he could play pretty much without thinking. That's when he met her eyes again, this time there was a hint of a smile. She was taller and older than the others, late thirties Leo guessed, ash blonde hair tumbling down over one shoulder and pushed back over the other. Simply dressed in jeans, tee shirt, a tasselled scarf and a little high waisted corduroy jacket that accentuated her long legs, she looked casually classy. She was slightly masculine in appearance, high cheekbones, broad shoulders, small breasts and slender body and the most amazing cornflower blue eyes. Leo came to the end of his set and gave a little smile in her direction as he finished. She returned it with a barely discernible nod. He decided to roll a cigarette, excused himself to Liam and headed for the front door holding the cigarette. Maybe if she smoked, she'd join him, he thought.

Smirting they called it, a blend of smoking and flirting. Leo remembered when they introduced the smoking ban in Ireland. It was thought it would be difficult to enforce but despite a lot of opposition it was accepted without too much trouble and people happily went out and chatted to complete strangers while they smoked. There were stories of people who met their future partners this way and the government was worried about reports of young people taking up smoking because they didn't want to miss out on the action.

Anyway, she didn't come out.

Leo went back in and re-joined Liam.

She was at the bar chatting to the barmaid and presently returned to her seat with a drink.

They carried on playing and Leo's drink was getting low. At the end of the number Leo asked Liam if he'd like a drink.

'No thanks, I'm fine, I only drink tea when I'm playing, I'll have a dram wi' ye when we're finished.'

At that moment, the barmaid appeared and placed a pint of Guinness in front of Leo.

'There you are!'

'Oh! thank you,' said Leo.

'Don't thank me thank the lady over there,' she replied, nodding in the direction of the subject of Leo's admiration.

Leo gave her a smile, his heart pounding.

'You're doing well tonight,' said Liam, with a grin.

'Listen Liam, I'm going to play *Eleanor Plunket*, it's an O'Carolan tune, always breaks their hearts, I do it in D.'

'I don't know it, but I'll try to pick it up as you go,' Liam replied.

It was a beautiful tune, haunting but uplifting rather than sad, and Leo gave it all he'd got. They silenced the room with it and at the end got a hearty round of applause.

Liam did another song and then said to Leo, 'Do a couple of fast tunes and then we'll finish with *'Wild Mountain Thyme'*, they like me to finish about half an hour before closing time.'

So, Leo said to those within hearing distance, 'We're going to finish off now with a couple of jigs; thanks very much for listening to us and to those of you that have bought us a drink or put a few bob in the tip jar.'

They blasted away accompanied by much clapping and stamping of feet and when it was finally over got the inevitable calls for more.

Leo winked at Liam as he played the first few bars of *Wild Mountain Thyme*, the crowd knowing that this song signalled the end of the night. They took turns with the verses and the crowd joined in with the choruses, singing it three times at the end before finally applauding and returning to their pints, drams and conversations.

'I'll get you that dram, what's your tipple?' Leo asked Liam

'No, no, I'll get them out of the tip tin, we've done well tonight. So, what's yours?'

'Ardbeg, if they've got it, thanks.' Leo replied.

He decided to go over and thank the lady for buying him a drink, as some of the others were preparing to leave.

'Thank you for the drink, did you enjoy the music?'

'I liked the music and I liked you,' she replied.'

Leo was normally fairly cool, but he blushed and she laughed.

'Do you mind if I join you for a little while?'

'Not at all, the girls are just leaving, the seats are free.'

'Thanks,' said Leo, taking a seat.

The girls said goodbye in a mixture of foreign accents and the Canadian shook Leo's hand.

'Friends of yours?' Leo asked.

'No, just got chatting,' she replied.

Just then Liam appeared and placing two small glasses and a water jug on the table said, 'There you, go thanks for joining in tonight.'

'Very much appreciated.'

'You're always welcome,' Liam said and moving closer whispered, 'I'm going down The Oak after this, it's open late… join me if you wish.'

'I might do that, thanks,' Leo replied.

Liam made his way back to the bar.

'You know Liam then?' Leo's new companion asked.

'Just met him tonight, it's my first time in here… and you, are you a regular?'

'Sort of, depends who's on. I come for the music, it reminds me of home,' she replied'

'And home being?'

'I'm from Donegal originally.'

Leo was about to tell her he was from an Irish background when it dawned on him that he hadn't asked her her name.

'Oh, do pardon me but we haven't introduced ourselves. I'm Leo, Leo Coyne.'

'I'm Fiona,' she replied, 'Fiona Frielle, pleased to meet you.'

She looked at the glasses, 'I take it that's whisky.'

'The finest Ardbeg malt,' said Leo.'

'I don't usually drink whisky,' she said, adding a drop of water to it, 'but sometimes people up here give you no choice. Here's to meeting you!'

'And here's to meeting you!' Leo replied as they chinked glasses.

'So, you're from Donegal? Your ancestors must have come over with the Vikings.' Leo said and immediately regretted it.

'I suppose I do look a bit Scandinavian,' she replied without emotion.

'I didn't mean to—'

'It's all right,' she cut him off, 'and how about you?'

'I was born in England, but my folks were from County Mayo. They're dead and gone now, had hard lives. I got dragged over there every summer when I was a kid, one week at Dad's farm and one week at Mom's, same every year for about fifteen years. I still go over but travel around more now.'

'So, what are you doing in Edinburgh?' she asked.

'I'm thinking of moving up here,' he replied.

'Why Edinburgh?'

'I like the people, I like the place and there's a good music scene.'

'Fair enough, where are you living at the moment?' she asked him.

He thought for a moment. 'Birmingham,' he replied'.

'Got anywhere in mind?' she asked.

'Not yet, I'm going to start looking tomorrow, an apartment or tenement flat within walking distance of the Old Town would be ideal.'

The bell rang for last orders.

'Would you like another drink, or do you fancy coming to the Oak with me?' Leo asked her, adding, 'they're open late.'

'That's very kind of you but really I'd better be going,' she replied.

'That's a shame, look Fiona ...' said Leo nervously, 'could I meet you again?'

'Leo, I'd only break your heart.'

Leo looked into her eyes. 'It's already broken,' he said.

She smiled at him, she was silent for a while and then said, 'OK, give me your phone number and I'll contact you. I can't give you mine at the moment.'

'You're with someone else,' said Leo.

'I'm not actually but it's complicated,' Fiona replied.

She took out a pen and a little notebook from her handbag.

OK, fire away,' she said.

Leo couldn't remember his number and took out his phone, pressed 'own number' and read it out. She jotted it down and put the notebook back in her bag. Leo thought it strange that she didn't simply save it on her phone.

'Are you sure I can't persuade you to come to the Oak just for one more?' Leo tried one more time.

'Look,' she replied, 'I don't really want to go to the Oak, but I know somewhere else and its open even later.'

'Where's that?' Leo asked eagerly.

'The Banshee Labyrinth,' she whispered.

Leo rolled a cigarette.

'Could you do me one?' she asked.

'Sure,' Leo replied.

'I'll see you outside,' Leo said to her and went to get his fiddle case and say his goodbyes to the bar staff — Liam had already gone.

They lit up in the street and she took him in the direction of the Oak. When they came to it she stopped momentarily and then hurried past and headed down a narrow street that led down to the Cowgate. They crossed Cowgate and went up the street opposite where they found The Banshee with half a dozen laughing and smoking people outside.

The front bar was full of a noisy, boisterous crowd and there were no free seats, but Leo still ordered drinks. They both had Guinness, 'I suppose that reminds you of home too,' said Leo. They decided to explore and went down corridors that seemed like tunnels until they found a bar that resembled a cave. There was a small table and a couple of seats free by the wall, so they sat down.

'Well this is certainly different,' said Leo.

'I know all the best places,' Fiona replied, with a wink.

There was a singer with a guitar who was entertaining with ghost stories in between songs. He also sang three ghost songs, none of which Leo had heard before; *Sweet William's Ghost*, *The Ghosts of Culloden* and the particularly scary *The Prisoner of Spedins*.

He looked over at Leo, eyeing his fiddle case, 'Are you going to give us a tune?' He asked.

'Sorry, I'm played out but since you are doing ghost songs, I'll sing you the only one I know,' Leo replied.

'Good man!' replied the singer.

Leo took out his fiddle and tuned it to his voice. He played the melody of *The Lover's Ghost* once through, and then placed the fiddle on his lap as he started singing: 'Oh then welcome home again, said the young man to his dear…' He continued with the song and when it came to the words: 'Oh my pretty little cock, oh my handsome little cock, I pray you will not crow before the dawn,' a few people sniggered. When it came around again: 'But oh this little cock, this handsome little cock,' people were openly laughing.

'It's not meant to be funny,' Leo said, with mock indignation.

Leo continued with the song and the room quietened till you could almost hear a pin drop. As he came to the end a man on the other side of the room passed out and fell to the floor with a crash. He instantly came around and his friend helped him to his feet. Leo was not sure whether the man was drunk or had fainted. The barman called a bouncer and they went over to see what was going on. The man's friend assured them that he was all right but said he'd take him home anyway. They started to make their way out and as they passed Leo, the man who'd fallen said, 'It's him, I tell you, it's him,' pointing at Leo.

'Come on,' said his friend, 'I'm taking you home.'

'Do you know him?' Fiona asked Leo.

'I've never seen him in my life before,' he replied.

The barman returned to the bar, the lights brightened, and loud dance music came through the speakers.

'It looks like the live entertainments over,' said Leo.

'Just as well, I think I've had enough,' said Fiona, looking at their empty glasses.

'Let's give it another five minutes, give those guys time to clear off,' Leo replied.

When they left the street was clear and they headed up towards the Royal Mile.

Before they reached the busy streets, Leo stopped.

'Fiona,' he said looking into her eyes. It occurred to him that he was five-foot eleven and she was looking directly into his eyes, in heels she'd tower over him.

'Leo,' she said, 'may I kiss you?'

'So long as you don't mind the taste of old Virginia smoke and west coast whiskey,' Leo replied.

They kissed.

Leo felt like an eighteen-year-old.

'I'll have to get a taxi,' she eventually said.

'Do you live far away?' asked Leo. 'Not really but it's safer,' she replied.

'I could walk you home,' said Leo.

'Look Leo, I really like you and I'd invite you back, but I can't at the moment.'

'You *are* with someone else,' said Leo.

'I've told you I'm not and I will explain the situation to you when I can.'

'You could stay with me,' said Leo.

'What!' She said.

'At the hotel, I've got a double room.'

Fiona looked at him. She wasn't sure; there was work to go to in the morning and ... 'What the hell ... go on then.'

'Are you sure?' Leo asked her.

'We're adults, aren't we?' she said with a smile.

They turned around and hand in hand they headed back down the street.

Back at the hotel Leo emerged from the bathroom to find Fiona on the bed, sat cross-legged in just her T-shirt.

He joined her.

He started with a head massage and worked down.

'You don't have to do this you know, we've only just met,' Leo whispered.

'I need you Leo,' she replied and pulled him towards her.

Chapter 4

Leo woke and reached for Fiona, but he was alone. He sat up and reached for his watch from the bedside cabinet.

Shit! Nearly eleven o'clock and I've missed breakfast, he thought to himself. He got up and looked around the room ... no trace of Fiona. He'd slept like a baby and yesterday seemed like a dream. He noticed a screwed-up ball of paper in the litter bin, picked it up and unravelled it. It was a page out of a notebook with his phone number on it, strangely with a series of letters written above the numbers. Well, he thought, I'll probably never see her again,

He quickly got ready and checked the dining area, but the cleaners were busy vacuuming, he grabbed a consolation complimentary newspaper and disappeared into the street.

He hurried along the grim dark recess that is the western end of Cowgate, hoping to find somewhere still doing breakfast. He got to Grassmarket and found a bar-cum-café that was advertising all-day breakfast. He went in, found a table, ordered, and was eventually presented with the largest breakfast he'd ever seen, consisting of haggis, bacon, eggs, sausage, white pudding, black pudding, tomato, mushrooms, beans, fried bread, and a pot of tea. As he contemplated the huge feast, he thought about the day ahead. He really must visit some estate agents and start looking for a place, but the thoughts he could not get out of his mind were all about Fiona.

*****

Jean Anderson was cleaning up the house in preparation for the weekly family get together when the phone rang.

'Hello, Jean speaking.'

'Jean, its Jim. Listen Jean, I had a terrible experience last night,' said a distressed sounding voice.

'Calm down, I'm listening,' said Jean, 'What happened?'

'It was in the Banshee. I saw your brother's ghost!'

'And how much had you had to drink?'

'I wasn't drunk. It was him all right and the one that was with him was no more than a skeleton under her clothes.'

'And what time was this?' asked Jean.

'About one-thirty.'

'One-thirty in the morning and you weren't drunk?'

'Look, I passed out with the shock of seeing him.'

'You're trying to convince me that you weren't drunk by telling me you passed out?' Jean asked incredulously.

Jean had received an earlier phone call from her friend Heather, who told her about what she'd seen outside the Scotsman's Lounge, but she wasn't about to tell Jim this.

'So, what happened next?' she asked him.

'We were asked to leave and Mike, the guy I was with, made me go and he took me home in a taxi.'

'Jim, this 'ghost', is probably just a double of Kevin; they say everyone has one. Tell you what; Sean is coming around this evening. Why don't you join us, and you can talk to him about it?'

Jim agreed to go around that evening; they said their goodbyes and Jean hung up. She didn't know what to think. Jim, a friend of the family, was notorious for having one too many but Heather was a level-headed and generally reliable person. Still they'd talk about it this evening.

She decided to cook a chilli as there would now be seven of them, eight if her sister Claire turned up.

Jean and husband Andy had three children, two, Hannah (aged 21) and Joey (18), still living at home and the other, Helen (24) living with her boyfriend. Jean had fought hard to look after the family, taking bar and cleaning jobs to subsidise Andy's wages. Helen had been to university and now had a good job. Hannah was still at university in Edinburgh and Joey...well... Joey was Joey.

Since Kevin had died Jean became more protective of Sean, insisting he came around to dinner twice a week and making sure he was looking after himself properly. As she busied herself with the cooking, she couldn't help but think about Kevin.

*****

Leo had found Ribsby Peters, an estate agent that specialised in apartments and scanned the selection in the window but there was not a lot within his price range. He went in anyway and explained what he was looking for.

'You might have to set your sights a bit further out,' the smartly dressed dark haired woman told him, matter-of-factly.

'This one's walkable through the park or there's plenty of buses and this one's a really good price for Leith Shore,' she said, handing him a couple of leaflets.

Leo looked at the leaflets, 'Interesting,' he said.

'Would you like to view?'

'I'll get back to you, thanks,' Leo replied.

At that moment his phone sounded, indicating a text message.

'Excuse me,' he said and read the message: *C u at the Guildford arms 1pm. Fi.*

'Excuse me again, could you tell me where the Guildford Arms is?'

'Do you know the Café Royal?' she replied.

'Yes,' said Leo.

'Well its right next door ... but I don't think you'll find anything in your price bracket in that area,' she said, with a great big smile.

'Thanks,' said Leo, slightly embarrassed, 'thanks for your help.'

Leo went out into the street, looking at his watch. It was almost one o'clock now, but he wasn't far away, he knew the Café Royal all right, a must for any visitor to Edinburgh and he vaguely remembered an adjoining pub. He tried to reply to the message, but the number was withheld so he set off sharpish for Princess Street. He hurried down West Register Street, turned a corner, and entered the Guildford Arms by its impressive revolving doors.

He couldn't see any sign of Fiona so went to the bar and ordered a pint. He found a table, sat down, and studied the room. It truly was a splendid place with its ornate ceilings, arches and gallery restaurant. The clientele was mostly business types out for lunch or a quick lunchtime drink. He wondered if she was up in the restaurant but decided to wait a while before looking in case the staff thought he wanted to eat. The breakfast he'd not long ago had was enough to keep him going all day. He took out the leaflets from the estate agent and pored over the details. The first one was in Abbey Hill round the back of Holyrood Park. Nice walk in the daytime, not sure about at night though, thought Leo. It was two-bedroomed, first floor tenement and it was about the same price as what he would get if he sold his own place in Coventry. The downside was it didn't look too impressive in the photos. The other place was only one-bedroomed, and the price was quite a bit above what he could afford but it looked far more impressive.

'There you are!' came a voice from above him.

He looked up, he hardly recognised her in business suit, make up, jewellery and hair tied up in an elaborate style, only her eyes told him it was Fiona.

She sat down beside him, a glass of white wine in her hand.

'Fiona, I hardly recognised you.'

'What? Oh, this get-up, essential for the job I'm afraid, hate dressing like this really.'

'You look very elegant, what do you do?'

'Work in retail, look, sorry about this morning,' she said, changing the subject, 'had to dash and it seemed a shame to wake you.'

'That's all right, said Leo, 'I was worried that I might not see you again.'

'She took a sip from her glass. 'Well don't you worry about that, in fact I've a special treat for you, I've booked us a table at Il Pescatore, it's on Leith Shore, for tomorrow night. It's on me, be there at eight.'

She drained her glass, 'Must dash!' she said, kissing him on the cheek and was gone leaving just a waft of expensive perfume.

A thrilled but perplexed Leo finished his drink, she is certainly a mystery, he thought.

He decided to walk to the two properties and have a look at them from the outside. He would time how long it took to walk, and he could also check out the location of the restaurant while he was in Leith.

*****

Jean was humming to herself as she placed the wine and garlic bread on the table. Everyone had turned up and she was especially pleased that her sister, Claire, who she didn't see so often, had made it. Jim, an old friend of Sean's had also made it.

As she brought the rice in and a huge pot of chilli she called out 'Joey, come and sit at the table.'

'I'll have it over here Mam,' Joey replied.

'You'll come and sit at the table and leave that damn play station alone for ten minutes of your life!' Jean commanded.

'You heard what your mother said,' Joey's father spoke up.

Joey tutted and reluctantly joined the others.

They all began to eat, and Jean was commended for her culinary skills.

'It's a wee bit fiery,' said Jim.

'That's because I use fresh chillies but there's plenty of wine to wash it down, not that you need any encouragement Jim,' Jean, who was wee bit fiery herself, replied.

They all exchanged niceties about family, friends, work, and the weather. Joey, having finished, returned to his play station. The conversation inevitably came around to the sightings of the previous evening.

'Well, talking about family, I had a strange experience yesterday,' said Sean.

'I know, Heather phoned me,' said Jean.

'What happened?' asked Claire.

'Well first I went in the Grey Mare and they reckoned Kevin had been in there the day before...'

'I've seen him, I've seen him!' an animated Jim cut in.

'Let Sean finish!' Jean ordered.

'As I was saying, first I was told Kevin had been in the Grey Mare and later I met Heather and she told me she had seen his double. Now I didn't see him, but Heather did and so did the barman, oh and so did the man at the funfair.'

'The man at the funfair?' asked Jean.

'There was a vacancy with the ghost train and Kevin's double asked about the job,' Sean continued.

Helen looked at Hannah and started to laugh.

'I know it sounds ridiculous but I'm serious.'

'I'm serious as well,' said Jim, 'and what I saw was Kevin's ghost!'

Joey, who up until that moment was engrossed in his PlayStation game, pricked up his ears on hearing the words 'Kevin's ghost'.

'Come on now Jim, we all know there's no such thing as ghosts,' Andy spoke up.

But Joey thought otherwise, in fact he knew otherwise, although he hadn't told anyone, he'd spoken to Kevin through a medium and if Kevin's ghost was about, he'd find him,

'Well I saw him; he even sang a song about a ghost,' Jim continued.

Helen and Hannah could hardly contain themselves, but Jean noticed Joey had stopped playing, was rocking back and forth and listening intently, 'Joey,' she said, 'don't you be getting any daft ideas into your head.'

Joey said nothing.

'There'll be a simple explanation to all this and it's probably that there's just someone who looks like Kevin knocking about around Edinburgh,' Sean said. 'Funny though, how he seems to go to all the places Kevin used to go,' he added, wistfully.

Chapter 5

Leo awoke refreshed after a much-needed early night and fortified by a leisurely breakfast was back in the office of Ribsby Peters by ten o'clock.

'Did you find an attic room above the Guildford?' the dark-haired woman asked, by way of a greeting.

Leo was aware that she was taking the pee, 'No, he said, 'but I found something far more interesting and I'm not talking rooms.'

'Oh aye?' she replied.

'That would be telling, anyway I'd like to view the properties you told me about yesterday, if that's possible.'

'No problem, they're both with vacant possession, I can take you now if you like.'

'That would be great, thanks.'

She looked at him just a little longer than was necessary, he thought.

'I'll just need to take your details.'

Leo gave her his name, address and phone number and she tapped them into a computer. When she'd finished, he said, 'I didn't get your name.'

'Oh, sorry, its Sarah, I'll just go and get the keys.'

She returned with the keys and led him outside where a sporty hatchback was parked.

'Jump in, Leo.'

She drove him out towards Meadowbank through a sea mist which had rolled in and left the city shrouded in gloom.

'It's meant to clear later, wind's freshening,' she said, making conversation.

'Hope so,' Leo replied.

She pulled up outside the property and they got out. The main door was unlocked, and a short corridor led past two ground floor flats to a stone stairway with iron rails. They climbed the steps through an aroma of what smelled like boiling cabbage and it reminded Leo of those stays with his aunt in Glasgow long ago. She unlocked the door and entered the bare flat. There was a lounge to the right with an adjoining kitchen, a bathroom and toilet directly in front of the front door. To the left there was a decent sized bedroom plus a small room which you would struggle to fit a single bed in. The whole place was in a quite a bad state and would need gutting, thought Leo, but he could do it.

'I'm afraid it does need doing up a bit,' said Sarah.

'Yes, with Semtex!' Leo cut in, with a laugh.

'But you won't find anywhere else at this price round here,' she continued, giving Leo a cross look.

'Only joking,' Leo replied, 'I know it's a good price.'

'Well, what do you think?'

'I could afford it and I suppose I could cope with it but let's have a look at the other one, eh?'

They went back to the car and Sarah drove expertly through the side streets and along a road through the middle of a park.

'Pleasant,' commented Leo.

'Aye, Leith Links, it's just a short walk from the apartment,' Sarah replied.

'The entrance is at the back,' she said as she pulled down a little street off Bernard Street.

The old stone building stood elegant and proud, a relic of the days when Leith was an important and thriving commercial port.

Sarah parked the car with the bonnet under the wrought iron steps that led to the entrance door.

'Your own parking space,' she said with a smile.

They climbed the steps and entered a little corridor that passed a small but well-equipped modern kitchen and led into a huge open plan lounge. A large window ran almost the length of it and the mist outside was beginning to clear allowing a pale spring sun to light up the room. There were a few items of furniture left including a large oak bookcase along one wall. Leo inspected it.

'The last occupant left it,' Sarah said, watching Leo, 'probably too big to get out without chopping it up.'

'That would have been a shame,' Leo replied.

He moved through to the bathroom; everything was new and working. There was only one bedroom, but it was a good size and he could use half the lounge as a study and home for his musical instruments.

Sarah could see he liked it. 'A bit better than the last place?' she said.

'I love it,' said Leo, 'but I'm about twenty grand short of the price.'

'Well it's not going to come down ... you could always get a mortgage for the remainder.'

'I've not got any regular work at the moment,' Leo admitted.

'There's plenty of work in Edinburgh.'

'I'll have to see,' said Leo, his mind beginning to wander.

'Seen enough?' she said, 'only I'd better be getting back.'

'Yes, that's fine thanks,' Leo replied.

They made their way back to the car.

'Do you want dropping back in town?'

'That would be good, thanks.'

'Anywhere in particular?' she asked him.

'By your office is fine.'

They were back in no time.

'You know your way around Edinburgh?' Sarah asked him before they got out of the car.

'Only the centre, really,' he replied.

'Here's my card, give us a bell if you need any help.' She gave him that smile again, slightly patronising, the way you'd smile at a small child trying to do something that was beyond its capabilities.

'Thanks, I might just do that,' he replied, with what you might call an ordinary smile.

Leo thought about Sarah as he walked up the street away from her office. He quite liked her, and she would be useful to know. Under normal circumstances he would have definitely taken her up on her offer, but Leo was totally beguiled by Fiona.

*****

About the same time as Leo was looking at flats, Joey Anderson was walking into the misty city centre. He could get anywhere in Edinburgh in minutes on his skateboard or his trial bike but if he wanted to go inside anywhere he had the problem of chaining his bike up or carrying his skateboard into places and most places did not welcome a youth in a baseball cap and Celtic shirt, carrying a skateboard.

There are certain places in Edinburgh where it is not wise to wear a Celtic football shirt, but Joey did not care. Kevin had bought it him and Kevin had been his favourite uncle. Celtic was Joey's team and whenever they played at Hearts or Hibs, Kevin used to take him.

Now, Joey was on the trail of Kevin. Joey was special; the medium who had contacted Kevin told him so. She said he was sensitive, receptive and in tune with the spirits, whether or not this translated into stupid and gullible, Joey did not think so, but the medium cost money and he had very little of that. He would do it his own way.

He decided to start by visiting some of the places Kevin used to go to. First port of call would be The Greyfriars Bobby where Kevin would take visiting friends or relations, rather than to the dives he normally frequented. He loved to tell them the tale of the loyal Skye Terrier, Bobby, who stood guard at his master's grave for fourteen years until Bobby himself died and was buried alongside his master in Greyfriars Kirkyard.

As Joey approached the bar, he contemplated the entrance to the kirkyard and decided to have a look around there first.

A pale sun was fighting a losing battle to penetrate the shroud of mist but occasionally a sigh of the wind would reveal headstones looming into view and then disappearing as the mist settled. Joey ventured to the far side of the graveyard and as he did the memorials grew increasingly macabre, austere angels with trumpets, heralding glorious ascension to heaven and diabolical gargoyles warning of eternal damnation. Dancing skeletons carved in stone accompanied him on his way until he reached a row of open topped room-sized tombs. He entered one. The debris of shattered monuments littered the floor, as if thrown there by an angry devil, water drip-dripped down the slimy stone, a chill came over him as a skull grinned from the wall, but he was not afraid, and he knew Kevin was not here.

*****

Leo made his way across Princes Street and up The Mound, he was wondering about lunch, maybe a light snack or bar meal, he didn't want to ruin his appetite for his dinner date. He came upon Deacon Brodie's Tavern and attempted to look in through the side windows, but they were too high to see in properly, he stretched his neck and found himself looking directly into the faces of a couple seated at the window table. He quickly looked away and decided to pass on. The next place he encountered was The Greyfriars Bobby.

*****

Inside the warmth of The Greyfriars Bobby, Joey felt a lot better. With his mousy blonde hair turning to brown and freckled face, he looked younger than his eighteen years but had his ID with him, not that he ever bought alcohol, he ordered a Coke and sat at a window table. The tomb was colder than the weather but here the vibes were good. He thought about Kevin and could almost feel his presence. The medium had told him that in order to make contact with the spirits you had to picture them in your mind and then concentrate until you could picture them vividly. This Joey did and then he saw him! But this was no picture in his mind, this was for real! Kevin's face was at the window, framed by the mullions of its traditional construction. Joey beckoned him but in a second Kevin was gone.

Joey ran outside but there was no sign of him. Unsure which way he had gone, Joey ran down the street and then turned and ran the other way, but it was no good, he had simply disappeared.

Joey stood on the pavement, half excited, half disappointed, he thought for a while and then he knew what he had to do.

*****

When Leo saw the youth in the baseball cap beckoning him through the window, he immediately thought of his assailants in Carrubber's Close; he wasn't sure if this was one of them, but he was taking no chances. He took off at speed, dodging the tourists, shoppers and office workers on their lunch breaks and cut down a side street then up another street and was now standing at the back of a long narrow bookshop. The place was a treasure trove of antiquarian and second-hand books, old maps, prints and artwork waiting to be admired or read again and Leo loved such places. So much history and so much knowledge contained within and the smell of old paper, inks, paint, paste and board was addictive to him. The proprietor, reading a book at the counter, occasionally eyed Leo over his half-moon spectacles. Leo gradually worked his way nearer to the door, glancing out to see if the coast was clear.

'Looking for anything in particular?' the proprietor asked him.

'Got any ghost stories?' Leo replied, without knowing why, it was just the first thing that came into his head.

'Don't get me started,' the man replied.

*****

That evening Leo set out for Il Pescatore. Rather than walk he took the bus and was contemplating his dinner date. Living out of a rucksack meant he hadn't many smart clothes with him, his black jeans and reefer jacket weren't too bad, so that afternoon he'd bought a new shirt and shoes to compliment them. He'd habitually placed the *'Do Not Disturb'* sign on his hotel room door on returning and had his afternoon nap. Shaved and showered he was feeling good, if a little nervous. The bus dropped him off in Bernard Street and after a short walk he entered Il Pescatore on the stroke of eight. It was actually called Il Martin Pescatore, 'The Kingfisher'. The proprietors had recently changed the name in honour of the birds that had returned to make the Water of Leith their home once again.

A waiter came straight over to him.

'Can I help you?'

'Erm, yes, is there a table booked for a Miss Frielle?'

'Yes sir, table for two, over there by the window,' the waiter led him to a set table in a little alcove.

'Thanks,' Leo said and sat down. He didn't know whether to say Fiona Frielle or Miss Frielle and was relieved that the waiter didn't say Mrs Frielle!

He looked at the wine list and the specials board, which was mostly Italian.

'Would you like a drink while you are waiting?' a second waiter asked.

Remembering that Fiona had white wine in the Guildford he ordered a bottle of Moncaro Marche Bianco.

The waiter returned with the wine, 'Would you like to try?'

'Yes please.'

The waiter poured a small amount into his glass and waited.

Leo took a sip, 'That's fine,' said Leo, although he knew very little about wine.

The waiter smiled and left him alone.

Leo looked at his watch, what if she stood him up, he thought, no that's ridiculous, she'd booked the table, after all.

He needn't have worried. At that moment, the Fiona that he'd met in the Captain's arrived, casually dressed, and wearing little or no makeup but looking fantastic. She came over, pecked him on the cheek and sat down.

'Sorry I'm a little late, a woman's prerogative.'

'That's ok, I'm just testing the wine for you,' Leo replied.

He poured her a glass.

'Just the one then, I'm driving tonight.'

'Oh, why's that,' Leo asked'

'Busy day tomorrow, can't stay out too late.'

Leo looked disappointed.

'But don't worry,' she continued, 'I've got Friday afternoon and the whole of Saturday off. That will give us chance to spend some time together if it's ok with you.'

'That would be great,' Leo replied, visibly brightening, although remembering he had booked his return train for Saturday.

The waiter returned with the menus and after perusing for a short while, they ordered.

Fiona ordered something called Caprese for starters and Leo, Funghi Selvatica. Leo thought it probably meant mushroom selection, but Fiona informed him that Selvatica is Italian for wild. They both ordered the same main, Branzino al Vino Bianco which is Sea Bass.

The starters arrived.

Leo's was a variety of mushrooms in open ravioli parcels.

'This looks interesting,' he said.

'The food here is always delicious and never boring,' she informed him, 'anyway, how did the house hunting go?'

Leo looked at the little parcel of mushrooms on the end of his fork, probably porcini, he thought before eating it.

'Excellent,' he said, 'the food that is, not the house hunting.'

'Oh,' she looked at him.

'The first place was a bit disappointing, needed gutting really, but that's not the problem, it's just that, well …' He took another forkful, Ceps maybe, 'I just didn't get the right vibe about it.'

Well, you've got to go with your instinct, what was the other place like?' she asked him.

Leo picked up another parcel with his fork, ah! Chantrelles, he thought, he had no problem identifying these as he'd picked Chantrelles in the Leal Forrest and had been wild mushroom hunting on a machair way up in the far north-west.

'I fell in love with the place. Its only about five minutes' walk from here. It's got a huge lounge-cum study with a large window that floods the room with light and it's all in tip-top condition.'

'And the problem is?' she asked.

'The problem is I can't really afford it.'

'How much are you short?'

'Twenty grand and the estate agents say the price will not come down.'

'Twenty thousand, I could sort that for you.'

Leo's fork dropped from his hand and clattered on his plate. 'What did you say?'

'I said I could sort that for you.'

'You are joking!'

'Not in the slightest.'

'But you hardly know me.'

'Leo,' she said, with a smile, 'twenty thousand isn't really a lot to me you know.'

The waiter took their starter plates away. Leo gulped his wine down and refilled his glass.

'No more for me,' Fiona said as Leo was about to top her glass up.

'You really are a mystery,' Leo said.

'What about if I come and have a look at it Thursday afternoon? You can treat me to lunch first, since I'm treating you now,' she suggested.

The waiter served the mains.

'Ok, how about a pub lunch at the Sheep Heid?' Leo asked her.

'Good choice,' she replied, 'see you there at one o'clock?'

'Or just after,' Leo replied.

'And Friday night we could go to the Captain's, you could bring your fiddle with you; It would be great to hear you play again,' she continued, ignoring his remark.

'Always willing to please,' Leo said.

'So, what made you choose Edinburgh as the place to move to?' she asked him, as they continued their meal.

'I've been to many European cities, Paris, Amsterdam, Copenhagen, London, Dublin and Athens but Edinburgh is special to me. It's not about the buildings, the museums or art galleries or even the scenery. It's about the people, the characters. I've met professors and buskers, poets and bus drivers, writers and railway workers and musicians of every kind and they all have enquiring minds, are willing conversationalists and treat each other as equals whatever their station... and of course there are some very beautiful people in Edinburgh!' he smiled at her.

She smiled back, trying to look embarrassed but she was too cool to blush.

'When I travel,' he continued, I try to immerse myself in the local community. What I'm looking for is not on any map or in any guidebook or tourist brochure, it's the spirit of the place.'

'And you've found it in Edinburgh?' She asked him.

'I think so,' he replied, 'Dublin is pretty good but no, it's Edinburgh for me.'

They finished the meal and Leo drained the last of the wine.

'Want to go anywhere else?' Leo asked her.

'No really, I've got a terribly busy day tomorrow and like I said earlier, I'm driving anyway.'

'We could go somewhere within walking distance of your place for an hour,' Leo wasn't giving up and he thought he might get some clue as to where she lived.

'I can't, I really do need an early night. I'll drop you off in town if you like. Tell you what; let's have a look at the outside of the apartment on the way back.'

Fiona paid the bill and they left. Leo looked at the row of cars parked outside, a few hatchbacks, a Range Rover, and a Jaguar XK. When Fiona stopped at the Jag, Leo could not stop himself from blurting out, 'Wow! This is yours?'

He realised he didn't sound very cool, 'Nice car,' he added quietly.

'Jump in,' she replied. He sank into the sumptuous leather seat, showed her the way through the few streets to where the apartment was and directed her into the space marked private parking. She pulled up with the Jag's long bonnet under the iron steps. They got out, stood back, and looked up at the old stone building. Leo pointed out the large window, illuminated by the streetlamps.

'That's the one.'

Fiona scampered up the steps and stopped on the little landing outside the door. She leant on the rail looking down at him, 'Well it's classy from the outside.'

'It's even better on the inside,' Leo replied.

'I'm looking forward to seeing it,' she said as she made her way back down the steps.

They got back in the car and Fiona drove to Leith Walk, over Waverley Bridge, up Jeffrey Street to Cowgate where she pulled up outside The Minerva Hotel.

'See you Thursday,' Fiona said and kissed Leo on the lips.

'Fiona,' he said, they kissed some more, 'are you sure you won't come up for a while?'

'I've told you I can't, be patient, good things come to those who wait.'

Leo said goodnight and reluctantly got out of the car. He stood outside the hotel and watched her drive off, a mystery within an enigma, he thought.

A dark coloured Range Rover slowed as it passed him, as if to take a look at him. Leo wasn't going into the hotel, not for a while yet anyway. He was too fired up and with only three quarters of a bottle of wine spread over the evening inside him, he was ready for a pint.

The Royal Oak, one of Leo's favourite pubs, small, but a magnet for musicians and interesting characters, wasn't far away and he'd been meaning to go there since he'd arrived in Edinburgh, so he didn't have to think twice about where to go.

He entered the bar and ordered his pint. It wasn't packed but there were no free seats and he knew it would soon fill up. This was the place where other musicians went when they'd finished their own gigs. This was the place where restaurant and bar workers went after work, people who lived by night and slept by day. He stood by the wall, placed his glass on a small shelf and took in his surroundings. A session was in progress with a guitarist seated in the corner hosting proceedings. A man with several *mouthies* (harmonicas) sat next to him joined by a fiddle player and an old man in a woollen cap completed the row. Three girls sat on stools in front of them as if in adulation and a woman played the piano at the side of the room.

Leo thought about his evening with Fiona. Was she really willing to stump up twenty grand to help him buy his flat? If the car she drove was anything to go by, she was probably very well off, but she hardly knew him. What the hell, he thought, whatever happens I'm enjoying myself.

The old man in the woollen cap buttoned up his coat, nodded to the barman and made his way out. Leo eyed the seat, no one made a move for it, well there was only room for one, but what if it's the old man's seat and no one else sits there? He decided to ask the fiddle player.

'No, no, you're welcome, sit yourself down,' the fiddle player, a big man with long brown hair, a beard and a check shirt, told him.

Leo sat as close to the end of the bench seat as he could to give the man plenty of elbow room. The three girls turned out to be on holiday from Cork and wanted some of the action. They asked the guitarist to accompany them as they sang *The Black Velvet Band* and *Molly Malone*. Irish top ten, Leo thought, but then one of them then sang an incredibly sad song, *Skibbereen* and silenced the room. Leo joined in quietly singing the last line of each verse.

When the song was over the fiddle player asked Leo, 'Are you a musician?'

'What makes you say that? Leo answered with a question.

'You look like a musician.'

'You think so? … I do play the fiddle actually,' Leo told him.

'There you go then,' he said handing Leo the instrument and giving him little choice.

Leo was surprised, not many musicians would willingly hand their instrument to a complete stranger without having heard them play. He edged along the bench away from the door a little and struck up a set of reels which were soon accompanied by guitar, harmonica and vamping piano. Someone produced a bodhran from under a seat to bring order to those drumming the tables and whooping along. Leo got a big round of applause when he finished. He handed the fiddle back to its owner and thanked him.

'My name's Leo by the way.'

'I'm Tom; pleased to meet you, have you not got your own fiddle with you?'

'Left it at the hotel, I wasn't planning on coming here originally,' Leo replied.

'You're fairly good, you could get some gigs.'

'You think so?'

'Are you around for a while?' Tom asked him.

'A few more nights,' Leo replied.

'Bring it down tomorrow, it's going to be a good night.'

'I'll do that, I've got a free night,' Leo said.

'Come a wee bit earlier, it gets a bit crazy at this time of night.'

Leo offered to buy Tom a drink, but he declined so he asked Tom to keep his seat while he got another pint. The room had filled up considerably while Leo was playing his tunes and he had to squeeze his way through to the bar, but the barman spotted him and served him straight away. When he got back Tom had managed to keep his seat but there was hardly any room left in the pub. Still people piled in, instrument cases stacked up in the corner, another guitarist managed to edge himself and a stool into the session and even a trumpet player joined in. Tom was right, it did get a bit crazy at this time of night, but this was the Oak that Leo knew and loved.

*****

At about the time Leo was entering the Royal Oak, Joey was striding up Kirk Brae, a small rucksack on his back. He'd got what he needed: candles, cigarette lighter, a crucifix and a torch; his destination, Mount Vernon Cemetery. This was where Kevin was laid to rest.

He arrived at the tall, iron gates and they were locked. The side gate and railings were lower than the main gates but had nasty looking spikes. He looked at the iron scrollwork of the main gate and reckoned these would make handy footholds. He checked that no one was watching and was soon over. He proceeded to the middle of the cemetery where Kevin's grave was located and sat down on a bench under a huge cross. He unfastened his rucksack and took out the candles and crucifix. He walked over to the grave, shone his torch on the stone and then placed the crucifix down on the stone. He took one of the candles, played the flame of his lighter over the bottom until the wax began to melt and stuck it down on to the gravestone. He then lit the candle but immediately it blew out. It was a calm, almost still night but the gentlest of breezes would blow the candles out. He hadn't thought about this. He shone his torch around looking for inspiration and found it. There were glass jars containing flowers on some of the other graves, these would do. He carefully removed the flowers from four jars but as he returned towards Kevin's grave, he tripped over a surface tree root and fell to the ground with a loud crash as the jars smashed on a gravestone.

*****

Davie Grant's back garden overlooks Mount Vernon and he was out on his patio having a pre-bedtime smoke when he heard the sound of smashing glass. Bloody vandals again, he said to himself. He went indoors, climbed the stairs, and looked out of the back window where he saw the flickering of torchlight. He went back downstairs, picked up the telephone and pressed the numbers 999.

*****

Joey struggled to his feet and made for the bench. He sat down to review the damage. His face and hands were cut. He wiped the blood from his face with his handkerchief then tied it around the worst cut on his hand. Undeterred he got up and collected four more jars, this time putting his torch in one of them to illuminate his way. He returned to the grave and lit a candle in each jar. He placed one at each corner of the gravestone and the crucifix on its little stand in the middle. The lights of Edinburgh were glinting far below, and all was quiet save the rustling of a reedy Phormium plant. He heard something rattle in the distance but knelt down anyway and said his prayers. He knelt in quiet concentration thinking about Kevin and trying to picture him as the medium had instructed. Presently he called out 'Kevin, it's me Joey; I've come to talk to you.'

There was no response, only silence.

Joey tried again, 'Kevin, give me a sign.'

A sudden, blinding beam of light shone in Joey's bloodstained face.

A loud voice shouted 'Police! …Freeze! We've got dogs.'

Joey tried to make a run for it but was soon apprehended and cuffed. They led him through the graveyard and not for the first time in his life, the hapless Joey was bundled into the back of a waiting police van.

Chapter 6

After his night at the Oak, Leo was thinking about what Tom had said: 'You're pretty good, you could get some gigs,' and supposed that if he was going to move here, he'd need to find some work. That work would be entirely better if it involved playing music.

He'd had breakfast and returned to his room. He'd done a search on his phone, found an estate agent back home and arranged for a valuation on his flat with a view to selling.

That done, he was now compiling a list of all the Scottish songs and tunes that he knew. He normally played mainly Irish material but there is a lot of crossover in the music and some debate about which songs are Scottish and which are Irish with many songs travelling back and forth between Western Scotland and the Northern counties of Ireland. The Scottish influence is especially prevalent in the Donegal fiddle style. Leo once had the privilege of hearing Tommy Peoples, the great Donegal fiddle player, play a favourite tune, Hector the Hero, which is definitely Scottish, in a little pub in Lisdoonvarna.

There were quite a few tunes that Leo did not know the names of but that wouldn't matter. What did matter was that Leo needed to practice them, especially if he was going to make a good impression at the Oak. He started to play but became uneasy. What if there were others like him staying at the hotel that needed to sleep during the day? He looked out of the window and although it was mainly in shadow, he could see that it was a bright sunny day. Another thought occurred to him; I wonder if a licence is needed to busk in Edinburgh? He knew one was needed to busk on the London Underground and you had to book your pitch, but different places had different rules. He decided to go out and check the territory. If all else failed, he could always find a park bench.

Leo left the hotel, fiddle-case in hand, and made his way towards High Street. Lured by the sound of a trumpet playing, he found himself in the small paved area that led through from Blair Street to High Street. There, on the corner by an old Palladian church that now served as a market hall, was last night's trumpet player. Leo walked by and dropped a pound coin in his case. The trumpet player, while still playing, raised his eyebrows in a gesture of either thanks or recognition. He seemed to be doing quite well, there was a fair bit of money in his case and Leo didn't want to interrupt him.

Leo carried on along High Street, passing a piper, dressed in full regalia, who was probably making more money having his photo taken with tourists than from any appreciation of the music he was playing. Leo decided he would not be able to compete with these types of characters so park bench it would have to be. He called at a shop and purchased a pack of sandwiches and a bottle of water for lunch then made his way towards The Mound. He could hear another piper in the distance as he descended the appropriately named Playfair Steps. He passed the Scottish National Gallery and down to where the piper was playing. The piper had got himself a prime spot against the wall between the Royal Scottish Academy and Princes Gardens. Leo walked past him and into Princes Gardens. At 49% Edinburgh has the largest number of green spaces of any city in the UK and this dramatic sunken valley with the multi-levelled Old Town towering above it and the castle keeping watch from the western end is certainly one of the most impressive. He kept going till he was almost out of earshot of the piper, found a bench and sat down. He rolled a cigarette and relaxed for a while.

There was a good stream of people coming and going past him and eventually he took out his fiddle. He was about to close the case when he thought, what the hell. He took a five pound note out of his pocket along with a pound coin and some loose change and placed them in the open case. He left the case to the side of his feet and tuned up. He then played away, working his way through his regular repertoire, almost oblivious to his surroundings. People came and went, some dropping coins into his case, Leo smiling or nodding to them in thanks. Sometimes little groups of people would gather, listen to two or three of his tunes and give him a round of applause. He realised when this happened you had to pull something special out of the bag to keep them and increase more people's curiosity; he was learning fast.

Out of the corner of his eye Leo spotted two police officers coming down the steps at the far end of the gardens. He decided not to take any chances and take a break instead. He put his fiddle back in the case on top of all the coins and another fiver that had joined his lure. He pushed the case under the bench behind his feet and sat back to eat his sandwiches.

The officers passed him without second glance as Leo finished his lunch. He could just about hear the piper, Leo thought about him, this must be his full-time job, all day, every day, who knows, five, six, seven days a week; still he gets plenty of practice without the neighbours complaining.

He had an idea; he opened his case took out the fiddle and counted up the money. He'd made over £40; he pocketed most of it and left the case as it was when he started. He tried picking up the tunes the piper was playing. The piper kept the tunes going far longer than the usual three times through which gave Leo a better chance of picking them up. He was faring pretty well at this when he was interrupted by an American voice.

'Say, are you guys working together?'

'What?' Leo said as he stopped playing.

'I just passed the piper a few minutes ago and you are playing the same tune as he was.'

'Must be telepathy,' Leo replied, and resumed playing.

'That's pretty impressive,' said the American, tossing a coin in his case.

Leo had no trouble with the military marches such as *The Battle of the Somme* and *Athol Highlanders* but didn't really know the Strathspeys; he would have to learn up on them. The tunes that he liked the best were the airs and the laments and when he could just hear the lovely *Leaving Glen Afric* he had to join in. Two women dressed in tweed and tartan, stopped to listen and clapped when he finished, he then played *Hector the Hero* for them and on completion one of the women told him it was her favourite tune. She obviously knew her stuff.

'That's the tune I want played at my funeral,' she said.

'Well I hope that's a long way off yet,' Leo replied.

'He was one of us you know, Major General Sir Hector Archibald MacDonald, son of a crofter who rose through the ranks to become a General in the British Army but was never accepted by the establishment and hounded to his grave by them.'

'Is that so?' Leo never ceased to be amazed by the knowledge and opinions of people he met in Edinburgh.

'Yes, that's the Hector in the tune. Have you got a card?' she asked him.

'No, I'm not from around here but I'll be in the Oak tonight if you know where that is,' he told her.

'Oh! we know the Oak alright,' she said with a grin.

They both dropped some coins in his case.

'Lovely playing. May see you later,' they bade him farewell.

He'd done pretty well and decided to pack up. That's another thing I'll need to do, get some cards printed, he thought to himself.

*****

That morning Jean was slightly worried, Joey hadn't come home the night before. Now Joey often didn't come home, often stayed over at friends, there was no controlling him, but Jean worried like a mother does and Joey had been acting strangely lately.

The phone rang and Jean's fears were confirmed.

'Hello.'

'Hello, Mrs Anderson?'

'Yes.'

'Sergeant McLeod, Police Scotland.'

'It's about Joey, isn't it?'

'We have Joseph Andrew Anderson in custody and not for the first time.'

'Look, you've got to understand, Joey is a bit … a bit different, he wouldn't harm a fly.'

'We responded to a complaint about vandalism in Mount Vernon Cemetery and found him covered in blood, he tried to run off.'

Jean could imagine what Joey was doing in the graveyard, but it was pointless trying to explain.

'Anyway,' the sergeant continued, 'we had him checked over at the Royal, they put a couple of stitches in a gash in his hand, and then we kept him in here overnight. We'll be taking a statement from him before deciding what to do with him. Either way we'll be releasing him, this place is full to the brim.'

'I'll come and get him, where is it?'

'St Leonard's.'

'I'll be right over,' said Jean,' putting the phone down.

*****

Leo awoke from his afternoon nap and reached for the remote. He was not much of a one for television, but he liked to keep up with the news. After the news, he surfed the many channels and chanced upon a repeat episode of the comedy, *Father Ted*. He particularly liked the series as it was filmed in a location he was very familiar with and in fact he knew some of the people that had appeared as extras in it. This episode, centred on a visit to Ailwee Cave, was one of his favourites and featured Richard Wilson AKA Victor Meldrew of *One Foot in the Grave* fame.

So it was a cheery Leo that set out that evening, buoyed by the comedy of *Father Ted* and his own successful afternoon's busking.

He decided to give the Jazz Bar a try as he fancied a loosener before going to the Oak. He descended the steep stairway to the underground bar, sat on a stool at the bar and ordered a Guinness. A blues singer/guitarist was mid-way through the early evening slot and was seriously good. Leo looked around the room; all the table seats were taken, mainly by tourists taking advantage of the early evening free admission, Leo supposed. Their polite, restrained applause after each number never varied whether the song was average, good or brilliant.

The singer's witty observations and world-weary sarcasm were largely lost on this audience judging by their non-reaction to his banter in between the songs.

Leo was joined at the bar by a familiar face, the man who told him about the Innocent Railway. He was with a group of people, some carrying instrument cases.

'Hello, Leo, isn't it?' the man spoke quietly in his ear.

'Yes, hello err...James?' Leo wasn't sure if he'd got his name right.

'That's right; you found your way back all right then?' James said with a grin.

'Yes thanks, a remarkably interesting route and I would never have known about it if it wasn't for you.'

'Where you emerged from the tunnel is called Hermits and Termits, but I've never been able to find out why,' James informed him.

They all stayed at the bar and when the singer duly finished his set, all applauded, and as a few tables cleared. James and co took over one of them and invited Leo to join them.

'Sorry, but I'm just about to leave,' Leo told them.

'You should stay here,' James told him, 'my friends are playing later and it's going to be a lively night.'

'I'd love to, but I've promised to play at the Oak,' Leo said apologetically.

'Well come back later if you can, they're on till late.'

'Maybe I will,' Leo said and bade them good evening.

He headed for the door but there were three to choose from and he couldn't remember which one he came in by. He had a bit of a panic attack, opened one of them and climbed the stairs, but these bare stone steps were not the stairs he had entered by. He carried on anyway until he came to a lift-bar door. He opened it and surprised the singer and the barman who were having a cigarette in the doorway.

'You're not supposed to come out this way,' the barman told him.

'Just testing the fire escape,' Leo said, with a grin and carried on into the street though regretting not stopping and having a cigarette with them. They seemed like interesting characters that would have been worth getting to know.

He walked the short distance to the Oak and squeezed through the crowded pub to the bar. He got his drink and made his way to the spot where he'd stood the night before, putting his glass on the shelf and his fiddle case on the floor next to the wall. The session was already in full swing and there were no free seats, Leo would bide his time, people come and go all night.

Then it happened again...a woman about Leo's age came through the door, looked at him and shuddered. She quickly looked away and hurried to the far corner of the bar. She was followed by two women who looked to be in their early twenties. They joined her at the bar and kept glancing over in Leo's direction. When they'd got their drinks the two young women came and stood quite close to Leo. They were laughing and joking, and Leo couldn't help overhearing them talking about the Father Ted episode that was on television earlier.

Leo smiled at them and said, 'You watched it as well…it's my favourite.'

'Yes, it was brilliant,' the taller of the two, an attractive girl with long blonde hair, replied.

'It was filmed in a part of Ireland that I visit regularly, and I know some of the people that were extras in it,' Leo informed them.

'Our family come from Ireland originally,' the other one said.

She was a slightly smaller version of the other, obviously sisters. Leo thought.

'What part of Ireland are your family from?' Leo asked.

'Letterkenny, County Donegal, on my father's side and on my mother's side, a little place you'll never have heard of.'

'Try me,' Leo said.

'Laharcoe, County Mayo.'

'And what is your mother's maiden name?' Leo asked, intrigued.

'Consadigne, why?' she replied.

'My mother, she's gone now, her name was Consadigne, Mary Consadigne and she was from Laharcoe. She told me she had an older brother who ran away to Scotland before she was even born, TJ, I think they called him.'

'Mam, Mam,' they both called to the woman at the bar.

She made her way over.

'This has to be your cousin,' the taller one said to her, but she didn't seem to be listening. She just went straight to Leo, hugged him tightly and started to cry.

When she finally let him go and was drying her eyes, Leo introduced himself, 'I'm Leo, Leo Coyne and my mother was Mary Consadigne.'

The older woman regained a measure of composure, 'I'm Jean and these are my daughters, Helen and Hannah.'

Leo looked at Jean, it was strange, there was a familiarity about her, yet they'd never met before.

'Pleased to meet you, Jean,' Leo said, before turning towards the girls, 'So you'll be my nieces?'

'Yes,' replied Helen, 'it looks that way, Tom was our granddad, Thomas Joseph, and some people did call him TJ.'

'I cannae believe the resemblance, you're the spitting-image of Kevin,' said a wide-eyed Jean.

'Of who?' Leo asked.

'My brother, Kevin, he died just over a year ago. You've been seen by one or two people who thought you were his ghost,' Jean explained.

'So that's the reason why I've been getting so many strange looks.'

'Aye well, Kevin was very well known, but what are you doing in Edinburgh?' Jean asked him.

'I've been here a few times before; I came for the music originally and I've just got to like the place. I'm actually thinking about moving up here,'

'Really, you'll have to meet Sean, he doesn't live far away. I'll phone him,' Jean headed for the door clutching her phone.

'Who's Sean?' Leo asked the girls.

'Our uncle, mam's brother, so that'll make him your cousin,' said Hannah, giggling.

Next thing Leo heard a voice in his ear, 'It's nae guid bringing it if yer nae gonnae play it!' It was Tom, the fiddle player.

'Or are ye gonnae stay here chatting up the young lassies all night?' he continued.

'These are my nieces, actually,' Leo replied, with mock indignity, 'and anyway there doesn't seem to be much room.'

'We'll squeeze you in, c'mon over,' Tom told him.

Jean returned, 'He's on his way,' she announced.

'I've been asked to play,' Leo told them.

'Come on then let's hear you,' the trio chorused.

So, Leo duly joined them, and they did indeed squeeze him in. He tuned up and eased his way into the session. After a while, he noticed two men, one of whom was presumably Sean, had joined Jean and her daughters. They kept looking over and shaking their heads. Leo felt guilty about not being able to talk to them so decided to play a party piece set of reels and then excuse himself to get a pint from the bar. He lashed into the reels and when he'd finished, got a loud round of applause, especially from Jean and company.

He put the fiddle in its case and made his way to the bar, but Jean intercepted him, 'This is my husband Andy and my brother Sean.'

'Pleased to meet you,' Leo shook their hands in turn.

'I'm getting these,' Andy said, 'what are you having?'

'I'll have a Guinness please,' Leo replied.

'So, you are Leo,' Sean said, facing him, 'I can understand why people mistook you for Kevin, but you won't believe the trouble you've caused.'

'Who me? … How?'

'Well I've fell out with three people, a friend of mine's been kicked out of a pub and worst of all, Jean's son has been arrested.'

'I can't see how any of that's my fault,' Leo reasoned.

'Don't be stupid Sean, how could Leo know anything about Kevin?' Jean interrupted.

'Joey said he'd seen Kevin's face at the window of the Greyfriars Bobby, had beckoned him but he ran off. Was it you?'

'I saw a youth in a baseball cap appear to call me when I looked through the window, so I ran off because two youths in baseball caps had tried to mug me. I'd battered them with the fiddle case, so I wasn't taking any chances in case it was one of them,' Leo explained.

'When did that happen?' Sean asked him.

'The night I arrived.' Leo explained what had happened in Carrubber's Close.

Andy passed drinks over to them all and Sean continued, 'Anyway, Joey was arrested in the cemetery trying to contact Kevin, the police have accused him of vandalism and released him on bail.'

'They know what he's like,' Jean cut in, 'they'll let him sweat for a month and then let him off with a caution.'

'I hope he's all right, where is he now?' Leo asked.

'Grounded,' Jean replied.

'Anyway, Leo's thinking of moving up here,' she announced to the others, thinking it best to change the subject.

'Are you serious?' Sean asked Leo.

'Deadly, I've already looked at a couple of places and I'm seeing a woman from here,' Leo replied while starting to roll a cigarette.

'Oh aye,' Sean winked. Sean was a bit of a one for the ladies but was not seeing anyone at the moment. 'What's her name?'

'Fiona, Fiona Frielle.'

Sean's brow furrowed, 'You'd better roll me one,' he said in a low voice.

'Just going out for a smoke,' Leo announced to the group.

Sean followed him out and got a scowl from Jean.

Outside, Leo handed Sean a cigarette.

'I haven't smoked for three years,' Sean said.

'You'd better give it me back then; I don't want the blame for anything else.'

'No, I need a smoke,' Sean assured him.

Leo lit Sean's and his own cigarette.

Sean took along draw, exhaled, and said, 'Now then Leo, please tell me you are lying.'

'Lying? What makes you think I'm lying? I am who I say I am, and my mother was Mary Consadigne.'

'I don't mean that, I can see that you are family,' Sean told him, 'I mean about the woman.'

'Of course I'm not lying; why would I lie?'

'Describe her,' Sean challenged him.

'Tall, slim, ash blonde hair,' Leo began to describe her, but Sean cut in, 'Posh bird during the day, hippy chick at night.'

Leo nodded.

'Leo,' Sean paused, 'Fiona Frielle is one of Jake McCullan's girls. Now that might not mean too much to you, but Jake McCullen is mafia, big time. I know about this stuff, I've done time for the bastards, take it from me, Jake McCullen is the most dangerous man in Edinburgh.'

Leo was silent.

Sean continued, 'When you say you're seeing her, what do you mean, have you been out and about around town?'

'Yes,' Leo replied, 'three or four times and well, she's stayed overnight with me.'

'Leo, you are a dead man, you'll need a machine gun in that fuckin fiddle case when Jake's boys catch up with you and then I wouldn't give you much chance. It's been great to meet you but the best thing you can do is get your arse on the next train out of here and don't come back for a long time.'

Leo remained in a stunned silence. He had no reason to disbelieve what Sean was saying and began to think of things like why Fiona wouldn't give him her phone number or tell him where she lived. He also thought about that black 4x4 outside Il Pescatore, was it the same one that slowed down to take a look at him outside the hotel?

Sean took another draw on his cigarette and put the remainder in the small ash box that was fixed to the wall.

'Promise me you'll keep your head down and get out of here ASAP,' he said.

'Ok,' Leo said, nodding his head slowly.

'Give me your phone number and I'll come and visit you for a weekend sometime,' Sean instructed him.

They exchanged phone numbers and went back inside.

The place was buzzing but Leo could no longer enjoy the atmosphere, his stomach was in knots and his mind confused.

'You two have been a while,' Jean pointed out.

'Aye,' said Sean, 'I was just telling Leo all about Edinburgh.'

The night rolled on; they chatted about Ireland, family, and Leo's life. More drink was consumed, and it was getting late when a voice boomed, 'Ur ye nae gaunta gie us anither tune?'

Leo went back and joined the musicians. He played the sad lament *Fear a Bhata* (*The Boatman*) with all the emotion he could put into it. A lament for Fiona, he thought. It was getting near to closing time, but still more people piled into the pub, some in various stages of inebriation and others who looked like they were just beginning their evening out. He finished the tune and decided to pack his fiddle away for safety.

He re-joined the others at the bar and not long after Sean announced, 'Our taxi is here. Do you want to be dropped off anywhere Leo?'

'No thanks, my hotel is only around the corner,' Leo replied.

Leo drained his last pint and followed them out to where a black cab was waiting. It occurred to him that if he'd taken up the offer of a lift, they would not have all fitted in.

Leo shook hands with Andy and Sean, kissed Jean, Helen and Hannah goodnight and they all got in. Sean, who was last to get in, whispered, 'Remember what I told you,' as he got in and closed the door.

Sean waved them away and made his way down to Cowgate. When he reached the hotel, he placed his fiddle case on the ground outside and rolled a cigarette. He stood there for a while smoking and wondering what to do.

Leo did not sleep easy that night. A few hours after he had gone to bed, he awoke, sweating, and his heart pounding. He was having difficulty breathing so sat up in bed. He thought about death. Either this was a panic attack, or he had been drinking too much. I must give up smoking, he thought. He thought about the situation he was in; why do I always end up in trouble? Or is it just life? You can't have the ups without the downs. He took steady deep breaths and gradually calmed himself. After a while he began to feel a bit better and lay back down to try to get back to sleep. To calm his mind, he tried to think of beautiful places he had visited but found himself clinging to the top of a cliff or falling down a mountain in a landslide.

He switched to thinking about a favourite piece of music but a vision of an old friend, a whistle player from Sligo, was telling him about the death of one of his old mates, 'The best spoons and bones player this side of Donnybrook. His last words as he lay on his hospital bed were

'There'll be no more music.' *There'll be no more music*, the words kept echoing in Leo's head.

He tried to picture a beautiful woman or a comforting voice but all he could see was Fiona's eyes and all he could hear was Fiona's voice.

It was no good; he couldn't get back to sleep. He got up; thought about getting dressed and going out for a cigarette, thought better of it and put the electric kettle on instead. He made a cup of tea and armed with a bunch of brochures he'd found in the drawer of the bedside table, got back into bed. He propped himself up with the pillows and read the *Welcome to Edinburgh Guide*. While studying the *Edinburgh Gig Guide* with its vast array of entries in small print he nodded off. The next thing he knew he was waking up the next morning, still propped up by the pillows, brochures scattered over him and a half-finished cup of tea at his bedside.

Chapter 7

Leo made a decision; he would go back home the next day as originally planned. He'd been a fool with Fiona: it was always too good to be true and now he was in danger; but he'd keep his appointment with her, one more day wouldn't hurt, would it?

After breakfast Leo showered, shaved and dressed. He tidied his things, tuned his fiddle and put it back in its case. He left the hotel and walked up to Market Street where he stopped to withdraw cash from an ATM, looking over his shoulder as he did so. There were a few beggars seated strategically alongside but he wasn't worried about them. He gave them a few coins and set off for Duddingston, making sure no-one was following him.

After walking down Cannongate he entered the park at Holyrood and rather than climb Arthur's seat again or Lancaster Crags, he opted to follow the Queens Drive and Duddingston Low Road. As he came alongside Duddingston Lough he looked at his watch and as he was early diverted through a small gate in the metal railings where he spotted a bench overlooking the lough. He sat down and rolled a cigarette, and as a swan moved over the lough, he contemplated his impending meeting with Fiona.

At ten to one he rose and continued to the Sheep Heid. At the bar, he ordered a pint and asked for a menu.

'What's Wagyu Burger?' he asked the barman.

'It's Japanese beef, the best!'

'Better than Aberdeen Angus?' Leo asked him.

'I'd better not say that, had I?' the barman replied, with a wink.

Leo found a table in a room where clocks were watching him from every angle and when they all showed five past one, Fiona, hair down and long multi-colored scarf trailing behind her, came bouncing in.

Leo stood up and kissed her, they both sat down, and Leo handed her the menu.

'I'm going for the Wagyu Burger; I suppose you know what that is?' Leo said.

'I don't actually,' she replied.

'It's Japanese beef, meant to be the best,' Leo informed her.

'Well if it's good enough for you it's good enough for me.'

'Ok, wine?'

'The Chardonnay will be fine.'

Leo ordered the food and a large Chardonnay.

'Have you driven here?' Leo asked Fiona.

'No, I came in a taxi.'

The waitress brought Fiona's glass of wine to their table.

'Cheers!' Fiona raised her glass.'

'Cheers!' Leo raised his pint and took a sip.

'You don't seem very happy; have you been gazumped on the apartment?' Fiona asked him.

'No, it's not that but I've no interest in the apartment any longer.'

'Why what's wrong?'

Leo looked around the room then said quietly, 'I know about Jake.'

'What?' Fiona looked horrified, 'Who told you about Jake?'

'I can't say.'

'Look, I can explain, I was going to tell you when the time was right.'

The food arrived.

Leo thanked the waitress then said to Fiona, 'Enjoy your meal, we'll talk later.'

They ate in silence and when they had finished Leo went to the bar and paid up. He checked the courtyard before returning to the table.

'Fancy a smoke?' he asked Fiona.

'I'd kill for one,' she replied.

They took what was left of their drinks out to the courtyard, which they had to themselves, and Leo rolled two cigarettes, handed Fiona one and lit up.

He took a long pull on his, exhaled and said, 'I've been advised, if I value my life to get out of Edinburgh and stay away for good.'

'Who's told you this, Jake, or one of his men?'

'Neither, I'm hoping they don't know about me yet but I'm not banking on it.'

'Then who told you?'

'I'm not prepared to name that person.'

'So, what do you plan to do?'

'I've got a return ticket; I'm going back tomorrow.'

'Look Leo, I'm sorry I didn't tell you about Jake, but I was afraid. I'm just one of his slaves, he owns me, and he owns my life, the same as he owns many others. Going to the music pubs is my only escape from a world I've grown to hate and when I met you, well ... Leo, I think you are the best thing in the world. Leo, take me with you, don't leave me!'

'But you can't just disappear,' Leo reasoned with her.

'I could stay with you for a week, see how it goes, I could say I'm visiting my sister,' she gripped his hand under the table, 'Please Leo, take me with you!'

Leo looked into her pleading eyes and knew, despite the warnings, despite the danger, despite the sheer craziness of it; he would do anything for Fiona.

'Call a taxi,' Leo instructed her.

'Where are we going?'

'Waverley.'

'You're not leaving now, are you?'

'No, I'm going to see if I can get you a ticket on the same train as me.'

A tear trickled down her cheek as she leant over and held Leo tight.

*****

Fiona called a black cab, which soon arrived and dropped them off at Waverley. They went into Caffe Nero on the platform, ordered two cappuccinos and sat in two large leather seats at the far end.

'Are you sure about this?' Leo asked Fiona.

'Absolutely!'

'Ok then.' Leo disappeared to the ticket office.

He managed to get a reservation in the same carriage but not seats together. Something troubled him and on the spur of the moment he decided to also buy two anytime single tickets to Glasgow. He paid cash and returned to the café.

'There you are,' he said, handing her the single to Birmingham, 'same carriage but down the aisle a bit from my seat.'

'Thank you, Leo. I'd better go and pack then, shall I see you tonight?'

'Would that be wise?'

'No problem, we'll go to the Captains, bring your fiddle.'

'But what about Jake?'

'I'm a small fish in Jake's ocean. With the deal he's fixing this weekend, I'll be the last thing on his mind.'

They finished their coffees and went out to the driveway.

Fiona flagged a cab, 'Want dropping off?'

'No, I'll walk.'

'Ok then, see you tonight then, nine o'clock?'

'Five-past,' Leo replied with a thin smile.

*****

Leo emerged from the covered driveway on to Waverley Bridge and instead of going in the direction of his hotel he was drawn in the opposite direction by the sound of pipes and drums. He crossed Princes Street to the paved area outside the Register House where a young piper was playing accompanied by a drummer with a full drum kit. This was piping to a rock setting and it was impressive stuff, it certainly had drawn a large audience who were tipping generously into the piper's case.

There's good money in this busking lark, Leo thought to himself, especially if you do something a bit different but alas, not for me, not in Edinburgh anyway. He watched for a little while longer and then turned and slowly made his way back to the hotel, wondering what the hell he was letting himself in for.

*****

The taxi dropped Fiona outside her Meadows apartment but before she went in, she phoned Marie at the shop.

'Hi Marie, I've got to go away for a few days so I'm putting you in charge. Get Liz to cover next week; she'll be glad of the extra money.'

'Is everything all right?' Marie asked her, she'd noticed a change in Fiona's behaviour over the last few days but couldn't quite put her finger on it.

'Family bereavement.'

'Oh, I'm sorry, does Jake know?'

'Not yet, keep it to yourself for now.'

'Ok, you can count on me.'

'That's my girl, I'll see you when I do, Marie, bye now,' she said, ending the call, and deleting it from the call list.

Fiona climbed the stairs to her apartment with trepidation, for the aroma of expensive cigar smoke told her two things: Jake and trouble.

Jake was sprawled across the sofa, smoking a large cigar and sipping a glass of malt. He was watching a boxing match from the previous night on catch-up TV.

'Make yourself at home, why don't you?' Fiona scowled at him.

Jake pressed the remote and switched the huge flat screen TV off.

'Just passing time, anyway how's my precious jewel?'

'All right I suppose, anyway what are you doing here? I thought you were busy.'

'I'm never too busy to see you, dearie.'

'That's a joke.'

'Don't be like that, now come and sit down and tell me what you've been up to.'

Fiona went to the kitchen, poured herself a drink and reluctantly joined him.

'Now then, what have you been up to lately?' Jake asked her.

'Oh, the usual round of parties, meals out, jetting off to film premiers and the like,' Fiona replied sarcastically.

'Including meals out with a new boyfriend?' Jake's eyes narrowed.

'What?'

'Fiona, I'm not stupid, you of all people should know that Jake has eyes and ears everywhere in this city and beyond.'

'I don't know what you are talking about.'

'Does the Il Pescatore at Leith ring any bells?'

Fiona reddened.

'Who is he?' Jake demanded.

'Look, I hardly know him and anyway I'm entitled to social life you know, think about how I feel.'

'Oh, I do, Fiona and I've tried to fix you up with many a good-looking wealthy dude, but you won't have it, will you?'

'I don't want an arranged marriage with the mafia.'

'You've already got one sweetie and anyway I asked you a question, who is he?'

'Look, he was just a visitor. He joined in at the Captain's, playing fiddle, he was really good, so I bought him a drink. I often buy the musicians a drink. Anyway, when the music was finished, he came over to thank me for the drink. We chatted for a while and he offered to take me out for a meal.'

'…and you paid the bill,' Jake interrupted.

Jake had obviously done his homework, but Fiona was thinking fast.

'He wanted to pay but I took pity on him, he hadn't much loot, made his money from busking and the like.'

'What's his name?'

'Leo.'

'Leo who?'

'I don't know, I only got Leo.'

'And where's he from?'

'He said Birmingham.'

'Have you got his phone number?'

'No.'

'You're lying, give me your phone!'

'Look it was a one-off date, I didn't get his number, I wasn't planning on seeing him again.'

'Don't lie to me!'

Jake snatched her handbag and Fiona immediately regretted not giving him her phone as Leo's number was not on it.

Jake turned the handbag upside down and shook its contents onto the floor. The phone fell out and as he bent down to pick it up, he spotted the train ticket. He picked the phone up and put it in his pocket, then picked up the ticket and held it aloft.

'Planning a little trip, are we? Birmingham, single, seat reservation for tomorrow … don't think so. Get your coat, I've a different trip in mind for you, he said as he ripped the ticket up in front of her eyes.

Jake walked over to the balcony window, opened it and took his own phone out and made a call.

Fiona approached him, 'Jake, where are we going? I'll need to change.'

'You're fine as you are for where we're going.'

'But where are we going?'

'Basically Fiona, you are going nowhere, especially not Birmingham. I'm just making sure of that, that's all,' he replied. He stayed there keeping his eye on the traffic below.

After a few minutes he spotted the black Range Rover pull up below, 'Come on!' he said, 'Time to go.'

He grabbed her arm and marched her out, pulling the door closed behind them. Fiona was strong, but she was no match for Jake who easily forced her down the stairs. He opened the outer door and glanced each way. The Range Rover was parked directly opposite. One of Jake's thugs got out of the front passenger side and opened the rear door. Jake quickly bundled her into the back seat, following her in. His man got back in the front and the driver pulled away.

Another of Jake's men was in the back seat and hidden by the Range Rover's blacked out windows, he and Jake quickly got to work.

'You know what to do, Mattie,' Jake said, menacingly.

Mattie, a huge man with a shaven head and scar across his forehead, grabbed Fiona's right arm.

'Get your fucking hands of me!' Fiona screamed.

But Jake got hold of her other arm.

They pulled her arms behind her back and Mattie expertly looped a plastic tie-wrap around her wrists and pulled it tight.

When Mattie produced two lengths of cloth Fiona went for him. She lunged towards him and bit a chunk out of his cheek. 'You fuckin' bitch!' Mattie raised his fist.

'No! Mattie,' Jake ordered, 'get on with the job.'

Jake's huge hands held Fiona around the neck while Mattie gagged and blindfolded her.

Mattie, hand on his bleeding cheek, glared at Jake.

'Get over it, aye; we'll patch you up later. Anyway, I'm surprised you can feel anything, you know what they say, where there's no sense there's no feeling.'

Mattie knew better than to answer.

Fiona wondered if they were going to lock her away somewhere or even kill her. She tried to speak but all that came out was a muffled moan.

'Don't you worry my sweet, just co-operate and you won't come to any harm,' Jake said, not in the least bit reassuringly.

She tried to imagine where they were going. She could feel the car lurch to the left and right; feel the ups and downs of the gradients, the rumble of the tyres on the sets and then the smoothness of the tarmac.

Eventually, in what seemed like an eternity but was probably only about ten minutes, the car came to a halt. One of the car doors opened but she was still firmly wedged between Jake and Mattie. She heard what sounded like the jangling of a chain on iron gates then the car pulled forward a couple of yards, the car door closed, and they moved forward a short distance before stopping again. The car door opened and after a short pause she heard what could only be a roller-shutter door, not the almost silent action like that of the shutter in the window of the New Town Perfumery but a noisy clattering and squealing of what was probably a large and not often used entrance.

The car pulled forward again, stopped and the engine was switched off. She felt Mattie get out then heard Jake's voice.

'Come on and don't try anything stupid.'

Jake took a firm grip of her arm and pulled her out to where a waiting Mattie grabbed her other arm.

'Top office!' she heard Jake order.

She was marched through an area that smelt strongly of new wood, up a short iron stairway to a landing where she heard the jangle of keys and a metallic sounding door open. They took her through and sat her down on an office chair that moved on its wheels and rotated slightly as she landed on it. They took off the gag and removed the blindfold but left her arms tied behind her back. Mattie and the other man eyed her like vultures, but Jake just smiled. Thoughts of what they might do to her flashed through her mind; she was afraid, but a calmness came over her, there was no point in panicking.

'What now?' she asked, rotating the chair with her feet to face them.

'Now nothing,' Jake looked at her and smiled, 'You're just staying here out of harm's way.'

He turned to the other two, 'Come on,' he said, 'let's go.'

'But you can't leave me here like this, I need the toilet and I'm hungry.'

Jake nodded at Mattie and the other man to go.

'Give me the keys and wait at the bottom of the steps.'

'He turned to Fiona, 'There's a toilet in there behind you and tea and coffee in the room next to it.'

'And how am I supposed to do anything with my hands tied behind my back?'

Jake walked behind her, took a stiletto knife out of his jacket and flicked it open. He cut the plastic tie-wrap and spun her round, stopping her when she faced him. He held the knife to her throat with the point of the blade just pressing into her skin,

'You fuck about with me again; I'll do you in with my own hands. Understand?'

He slowly removed the knife and walked out, slamming and locking the heavy steel door behind him.

He clattered down the iron steps and as the sound of the three men's footsteps faded, she stood up and looked down through the barred window. There was very little light, only what was coming through the skylights and that from the single, unshaded light bulb that hung above her. She could just make them out, walking through a line of packing cases. They disappeared from view until car head lights illuminated the far side of the warehouse. One of the men operated the roller door, a dark vehicle drove out; he sent the roller door back down and disappeared through a small door at the side.

What light that had penetrated the filthy skylights had disappeared now and after the glare of the headlights had gone the warehouse was in darkness, save the long shadows cast by the solitary light bulb above her.

She turned to inspect the place where she would be incarcerated for god knows how long. A grotty toilet with no light, she had to leave the door slightly ajar, and a room with a camp bed, strewn with old blankets. She kicked the wall; it gave out a metallic clang. The whole place was of a steel construction, the type you might find on a building site, designed to prevent anyone breaking in – or out. It might have been an office once, but now it was nothing more than a prison cell.

She tried the door, no chance of forcing that. She looked at the off-white corkboard ceiling, strip light fittings were fixed to it, but their tubes had been removed. She stood on the chair, steadying herself as it rotated slightly and pulled away a panel but there was only steel above it. As she carefully stepped back down, she resigned herself to the fact that there would be no escape from this metal prison. She looked again through its barred window, there was no point in trying to break its toughened glass as the bars would prevent her escape anyway.

In the back room, she found an ancient electric kettle which she filled from the cold tap. There wasn't much else, a box of tea bags, a jar of instant coffee and a selection of grimy, cracked mugs. At least the kettle worked. She rinsed out one of the mugs with the boiling water, scraped a spoonful of coffee from the half-solidified contents of the jar to make what was possibly the worst cup of coffee she'd ever tasted. Not the speciality Cappuccino or Mocha that she was accustomed to but at least it was hot and she needed to keep warm.

Not knowing when she would eat again made her realise she would also need to conserve energy.

She eyed the camp bed.

The thought of lying under those old blankets instead of the fine Egyptian cotton sheets of her own bed disgusted her.

Nevertheless, she took one of the blankets and spread it over the camp bed and over the old cushion that served as a pillow.

She tied her long scarf around her head several times, forming a kind of hood, then, fully clothed, got on to the camp bed and pulled the remaining two blankets over her.

She thought about Leo. He would turn up at the Captain's even though he was worried about going and she wouldn't be there. He'd probably go home tomorrow as planned and she'd never see him again, although she had memorised his phone number and could contact him if she ever got out of this mess.

She thought about the life she had here in Edinburgh, the money, the flash car, the fancy apartment. They were worth nothing now, if they ever were, if she ever got the chance she would run, run, run away from all this for ever.

She drifted into sleep, dreaming about her home far away, in Donegal.

*****

Replenished by an afternoon nap and an evening meal at the hotel, Leo set out for the Captain's bar. He felt good physically but was full of a sense of foreboding. Surely Fiona was known in the place and tongues would wag, calls would be made, or text messages sent.

He had his fiddle with him as requested but for various reasons was hoping he wouldn't have to play. On arrival outside the bar he placed the case on the ground next to the pub wall and lit a pre-rolled cigarette. He studied the posters publicising each night of the week; tonight there was to be a band on, indeed, as a punter came out he was relieved to hear drums, bass and electric guitar sound checking, thinking there'd be no call for a diddley-dee fiddle player tonight.

With a nod and a quiet, 'Hi,' he politely acknowledged the grey haired, bearded man who had come out for a smoke.

Leo then turned his eyes to the William McGonagall memorial plaque: *William McGonagall, poet and tragedian died here 29 September 1902,* it stated. As he studied it, he could feel the grey-haired man watching him. Leo turned and put out his cigarette, and the man's eyes followed him as he entered the pub.

Leo ordered a pint from the barman. The jovial barmaid from earlier in the week was nowhere to be seen. He found a table near the window and looked at his watch. It was just turned nine o'clock, Fiona would come in any minute now ... only she didn't.

The door opened. Leo looked up, but it was the man with the grey hair and beard. He walked up to the bar, drained the remains of a pint, ordered another one and a dram and came and sat at the end of Leo's table.

He caught Leo's eye, 'I saw you looking at Willie Mac's plaque, are you interested in him?'

'Not particularly,' Leo replied, 'I don't know much about him really, I've heard of the *Tay Bridge Disaster* and that he's meant to be the world's worst poet, but I know more of Burns because of his songs.'

'You should nae mention Burns and McGonagall in the same breath!'

'No offence intended,' Leo assured him.

'They both wrote poems about Edinburgh, you know, now consider a verse from Burns.'
He recited,

'Thy sons, Edina, social, kind,
With open arms, the stranger hail;
Their views enlarg'd, their lib'ral mind,
Above the narrow, rural vale:
Attentive still to Sorrow's wail,
Or modest Merit's silent claim;
And never may their sources fail!
And never envy blot their name!'

He took a deep breath and sighed, 'Now compare a verse from McGonagall,'

'Then, as for Salisbury Crags, they are most beautiful
to be seen,
Especially in the month of June, when the grass is
green;
There numerous mole-hills can be seen,
And the busy little creatures howking away,
Searching for worms among the clay;'

Leo couldn't help but laugh, 'Perhaps McGonagall was satirising Burns' sycophantic praise.'
'I don't think so,' the man replied, 'McGonagall wrote a poem in praise of Robbie Burns, he would nae ken what satire was, although there is plenty of it unintended in his work.'

Leo looked at his watch, it was nearly nine-thirty.

Leo's new companion noticed, 'Are you expecting company?'

'Possibly… are you a scholar of Scottish poetry?' Leo returned to the subject.

'I'm interested in all things Scottish, my names Alex, I work at the museum.' He offered his hand.

'Leo; pleased to meet you, are you a professor or something like that?' Leo shook his hand.

'No nothing like that, guide and security, spend most of the day standing about.'

'Are you at the National Museum?'

'Aye, Chambers Street, the place is full of treasures, but most people spend more time looking at the Hillman Imp than anything else.'

'Ha! I remember the Imp, rear engine, not a bad little car. How come there's one in there?'

'They were built out at Linwood, a government grant supported project, supposed to provide jobs for the redundant steel and shipyard workers. Thus, it has its place in Scottish history.'

Alex knocked back his dram and washed it down with a gulp of beer. He continued, 'Trouble with the job is, like a coach driver or a barman, you're always waiting for your next cigarette break, it's hard to give up.'

He took out his cigarette packet, tapped it on the table, 'Excuse me,' he apologised and headed for the door.

Leo looked at his watch again, no sign of Fiona. Something was wrong he thought; perhaps Jake was on to her and perhaps Jake would come looking for him. He looked at his almost empty glass and decided to have one more then go, giving Fiona a bit more time to show up, but he wasn't over optimistic.

As he stood at the bar Alex returned.

'Can I get you a drink?' Leo offered.

'Thanks, but no, I'm off to the local just now,' Alex declined, grabbing the remainder of his pint from the table.

'Oh! Where's the local?

'Sandy Bell's, ye ken it?'

'Yes,' Leo replied, 'I might join you later.'

Alex drained the last drop and placed his glass on the bar.

'Please do, bye now and nice talking to you.'

Leo returned to his seat with a fresh pint. It was after ten o'clock now and still no sign of Fiona, he resigned himself to the fact she would not be coming now.

While talking to Alex he had become oblivious to the music but now listened to the band that had somehow squeezed themselves into the small area where he and Liam had played. Rock music with a Scottish and Irish flavour: Van the Man's *Brown Eyed Girl*, songs from the

Proclaimers, Franz Ferdinand, Snow Patrol, the Saw Doctors and Thin Lizzy were his soundtrack as he finished his pint and disappeared into the night.

Chapter 8

The clattering of heels on iron steps woke Fiona with a start, a key clicked in the lock, the door opened and banged shut again. Fiona sat bolt upright on the camp bed. In the gloomy light she could just make out Crina, one of Jake's street girls.

'Crina?' Fiona looked at her quizzically.

'It is ok Fiona, I have brought you breakfast and coffee. Jake, he wants to punish you, not starve you to death,' Crina assured her in her Eastern European accent.

Fiona struggled to her feet, unwrapped the scarf from around her head and splashed her face with cold water from the tap. She felt terrible and was glad she wasn't wearing make-up.

Crina produced a baguette and two cartons of coffee from a carrier bag and placed them on the small office table. She looked down at the one chair and then up at Fiona.

'No, you sit down, I need to stretch my legs,' Fiona instructed her before she had chance to speak.

Fiona removed the sizeable breakfast baguette from its container, 'Thanks, Crina, I need this, I'm absolutely starving,' she said, tearing into it like a person who hadn't eaten for days.

When she'd finished, she took the lid off one of the coffees, it was as though Crina was waiting for her before she took her own.

'I have brown sugar if you like,' Crina fished out a couple of paper tubes.

Fiona didn't normally take sugar but ripped the end of one of the tubes, letting the granules settle on the frothy top of the still quite hot coffee.

Fiona knew Crina from a few years back and had once stepped in to plead for her when she was sure Jake was going to kill her for supposedly double crossing him.

It wasn't until Fiona had taken a sip of coffee and was about to ask her what would happen next, that she'd looked at her properly. Crina's long dark hair partially concealed cuts to her cheek and forehead and the swelling around her right eye would surely soon become discoloured into a shiner of a black eye. Fiona stood up, 'Crina, what the hell has happened to you?'

'One of the punters got violent.'

'When?'

'Last night.'

'Does Jake know?' Fiona was thinking fast.

'Not yet, but when he does there's going to be another body found washed up on the shore of the Forth.'

'Crina, you've got to help me.' Fiona looked hard into Crina's eyes.

'You know I can't, Jake would kill me.'

'Not if he thought I'd tried to kill you.'

'What are you trying to say?'

'Look, I've attacked you with the chair, knocked you out, taken your keys and escaped.'

'But…' Crina began to protest.

'Crina, you look the part, I'll leave you with your phone, just give me an hour.'

'Fiona, I can't.'

'Crina, I saved your life once! You owe me one.'

'Ok, I'll do it, but I'm afraid.'

'Don't be, it'll be me he'll want to kill after this.'

Fiona downed the remainder of her coffee in one.

'You'll have to give me the keys, just the ones for this place.' Fiona held her hand out.

Crina reluctantly handed over the keys, Fiona read the fob marked *The People Warehouse*, pocketed them, and picked up the chair.

'Bloody hell, this is heavy.'

Crina looked at her warily.

'It's all right, I'm not going to use it, you've got enough injuries as it is,' Fiona assured her.

Fiona inspected the chair, it had five chrome plated legs with casters. The legs were attached to a stout metal central shaft that would be enough to kill someone if aimed at the right place.

'Right Crina get on the floor, you've got to be in a position where it looks like you've been struck by the chair,' Fiona instructed her.

On the floor, Fiona manipulated Crina's position until she looked like she'd been knocked to the ground. She placed the upturned chair close to Crina's head.

'That'll do, remember this position, give me an hour then get down like this. Then you can phone Jake. Make out you are going in and out of consciousness, drop the phone mid-sentence, got it?'

'I think so,' Crina struggled to her feet.

Fiona kissed her then hugged her tightly, 'Good luck, we'll both need it.'

Fiona took out the keys, one of them was particularly sharp. She looked at it for a moment then slashed it across her own thumb. Ignoring the pain, she squeezed her thumb and smeared the blood on the base and on one of the chair legs. She turned to smear blood on Crina's clothes and face, 'Blood sisters!' she said with a grim smile.

She took out a small handkerchief from her pocket and tied it tightly around her thumb.

'We may never meet again Crina, so thanks for this,' Fiona kissed her again, unlocked the door, stepped out of the cabin and to be on the safe side, locked the door behind her.

She crept down the iron steps and was making her way along a gangway among rows of packing cases when she heard the sound of an engine and air brakes. She stopped dead in her tracks as she heard a door being unlocked. She hid behind a packing case and watched as a man appeared through the small door, pressed the button and raised the roller door. A curtain-sider lorry drove in and pulled up with a hiss of brakes. The engine died and two men jumped out. The man on the door returned the roller to its closed position, switched on a couple of lights and walked across to where a fork-lift truck was parked. He started it up and drove towards the lorry where the other men were busy rolling up its covers, revealing a load of packing cases on pallets. He raised the forks, inserted them under the end pallet and removed it from the lorry. Fiona watched as he manoeuvred the truck around and trundled down the gangway in her direction. Worried that she might be discovered, she silently inched around the packing case that she was hiding behind, but he stopped short and deposited the load in a space almost next to her. She breathed a sigh of relief as he returned along the gangway without spotting her.

The next packing case was unloaded but just placed on the floor next to the lorry. Two men set to work opening it with crowbars. Fiona watched incredulously as five young women and two young men of North African appearance were led out. Although they outnumbered their captors, they obediently followed them to the other side of the warehouse where a row of Portakabins, similar to the one Fiona had spent the night in, awaited them. The parents of these poor refugees had probably paid people smugglers good money to unwittingly send them to a life of prostitution and slavery, Fiona thought to herself. People Warehouse? This was Jake's own private prison.

But now was her chance to escape. She tip-toed along the back of the packing cases until she was a short distance from the lorry. The men were allocating the cabins as she darted from behind the last packing case to the back of the lorry and from there to the small door next to the roller door. She turned the Yale type lock, stepped out and gently pulled the door to, hoping they hadn't heard her.

She was in a yard; there was a black Nissan SUV parked inside the open gates and a red Vauxhall hatchback outside. She looked at the chain and padlock hanging loosely around one gate. The padlock was a Chubb brand with an off-centre keyhole. She checked the keys and found one with an off-centre bit. She closed the first gate and aligned the second, dropping a locking bar into a hole in the ground. She then unlocked the padlock, threaded the chain through the two gates and locked it again.

The early morning air was chilly and clouds scudding across the sky above her brought occasional squally showers as she made her way along a road lined with industrial units, some in use, some derelict. On nearing the end of this road, she heard the roar of a fast-approaching car engine and instinctively dodged behind a gatepost and watched as a dark coloured Range Rover sped past.

Jake! She thought. Either Crina had panicked and called him or he was going there anyway to meet his men.

Once the car was out of sight, Fiona strode hurriedly on through streets she did not recognise until she reached a bridge that was blocked off to traffic by a row of bollards. A cast iron sign informed her that it was built in 1886. She looked down through its railings to where a river flowed below. Water of Leith, she supposed, as she dropped the keys with a plop and watched them disappear into its murky water.

She continued through the streets of a modern housing development until she came to a busier road, one she recognised, Great Junction Street. She hurried along to where it joined Leith walk, feeling slightly safer as there were more people about, and felt better still when she reached *Sahid's Supastore* where Barsha, an old friend, ran the family business.

'Fiona! What on earth has happened to you, you look terrible?' asked a shocked Barsha.

'Don't ask, I'll explain later, just lend me your phone for a minute, oh, and could I scrounge a cigarette?'

Barsha got a pack from the shuttered cabinet, 'On me,' she said, handing them to Fiona. She noticed that Fiona didn't have a bag, 'Need a lighter?'

'You're an angel,' Fiona replied.

With no customers in the shop to deal with, Barsha led Fiona through a door at the back that led to a tiny yard and left her.

Fiona lit up, took a long drag on the cigarette, and dialled the number she had memorised using letters to represent the numbers. The number rang, she took another drag of the cigarette while she waited and then it was answered.

'Leo, it's Fiona, you've got to help me!'

*****

The Range Rover pulled up at the locked gates. Crina's red Vauxhall Corsa was parked outside and a black Nissan SUV, which Jake knew belonged to Ray Morrison, was parked in the yard.

Jake, Mattie and Donal, the driver, all got out.

Jake inspected the lock and chain.

'Shit! Why have they locked it?' He said looking at Mattie. 'Have you got your keys?'

'No, I gave them to Ray, where are yours?'

'Crina's got mine and her car's here outside the gates, something's not right here.'

Jake called a number on his phone.

'What the fuck's going on?' he demanded.

'Nothing's going on, everything's going to plan,' a voice replied.

'Then why have you locked the gates?'

'I haven't locked the gates…'

'Don't piss me about, Morrison, get your arse out here and open them!' Jake ended the call.

'Do they know about Fiona?' Mattie asked Jake.

'Well I haven't said anything, but they might have discovered her.'

Ray appeared from the side door and walked up to the gates, looking at them in disbelief.

'I honestly have not locked these gates.'

He pulled the padlock through the gate bars using the chain.

'See, it's been locked from the outside.'

He unlocked it and swung open one of the gates. Jake brushed past him followed by Mattie and Donal.

They entered through the side door. Jake ignored the two men who had by now finished locking up their 'guests' and marched straight towards the office where he'd left Fiona the night before. Mattie and Donal followed, struggling to keep up with him. He stomped up the steps and grabbed the office door handle. It was locked. He peered through the glass in the top of the door to see Crina slumped on the floor with the chair lying on top of her.

He turned around and shouted, 'Ray, over here, bring the keys!'

Ray hurried over, took the steps two at a time and quickly unlocked the door.

Crina lay on her back, the chair on its side with its chrome legs across her neck. Her right arm was stretched out to where her phone lay just out of reach, as though she'd dropped it. Her eyes were closed, her face bloody and bruised. Jake could not believe it.

'The fuckin' bitch Fiona, I didn't think she had it in her,' Jake said as he lifted the chair off her.

'Crina! Crina…' he gently shook her.

'Whe… where am I?' she stuttered.

'Crina what happened to you? Did Fiona do this to you?'

'I… I don't know.'

Jake and Donal lifted her to her feet, she was very unsteady. They sat her on the chair.

'Don't worry, love, everything's going to be all right,' Jake tried to sound comforting.

He looked at Donal.

'She's obviously in shock, look at the state of her, you and Ray, get her to a doctor, our doctor.'

They got her to her feet again, helped her down the stairs and walked her across the warehouse to the yard door.

'Just a sec,' Jake said putting his hand in her jacket pocket and pulling out her car keys, 'Second thoughts, Donal you take her, you can drive her car, Ray's got business here and I doubt Mattie would fit in a Corsa.'

Crina, flanked by Donal and Mattie, felt quite well, out in the bracing air but whenever Mattie or Donal lessened their hold she made to fall. She had to keep the pretence up now, for her own sake as well as Fiona's.

They reached the car and Jake opened the passenger door. Mattie and Donal eased Crina in and Donal walked around the car to the driver's side. He got in, Crina was lying back with her head to one side like a rag doll. He reached over and pulled the seatbelt over her, straightening her up as best he could.

Jake and Mattie watched as Donal drove away then headed back into the yard.

'She's gone too far this time,' Jake said with a frown, 'When I catch that bitch, I'll kill her!'

Before Mattie could say anything, Jake's phone rang.

Mattie stood watching him take the call and saw his face light up.

'They've found lover boy,' Jake said to Mattie as he continued the call, 'Ok, good, ok, I'll call back ASAP once I've made the necessary arrangements.'

He looked at Mattie, 'This Leo fellow is staying at the Minerva, he's still there, we've got a man watching the place. We've obtained a staff pass from one of our girls who works there, and it's not a smart system. We need to move fast, Mattie.'

Jake made several more phone calls, getting his men to cover Waverley and Haymarket stations, especially Birmingham bound trains, and put an alert out for all his taxi drivers to look out for Fiona, although he doubted she'd be stupid enough to use one of his.

He then phoned The Choirboy.

Arnold Wilberforce was a pillar of his local community, a paragon of respectability, he sang in the church choir. Lean and fit, he ran marathons for charity and was always generous in helping local causes. Living in a big house out at Cramond, to his neighbours he was a stockbroker, but to Jake McCullen he was his highest paid and best killer. Jake called him The Choirboy.

One of Arnold's mobile phones rang. Arnold knew who it was.

'Hello Jake, what can I do for you?'

'I've got a job for you, right away, fellow named Leo, he's staying at the Minerva Hotel, room 121 on the third floor.'

'What's the problem, Jake?'

'He's been messing around with Fiona and now she's gone missing.'

'You want me to put the frighteners on him?'

'No, finish him off. Quick and clean, I want to teach that bitch a lesson.'

'You're joking.'

'I'll pretend I didn't hear you say that,' Jake paused, but Arnold did not speak, 'Mattie is on his way out to you now, we've got you a staff pass – opens all doors, the system's not computerised so it won't be flagged. Use the service entrance, there's no CCTV on it. There's a back stairway just inside. He always puts a '*Do Not Disturb*' sign on the door when he's in his room. We need to move fast before he checks out. Everything understood, Arnold?'

'Understood, Boss.'

'Now I'm hearing you!' Jake said, and ended the call.

*****

At last Joey was free. After a night in a police cell and two days and nights grounded at home, he had managed to persuade his parents that he needed exercise and some fresh air. They agreed to let him go for a ride on his bike so long as he promised to be back for lunch. Joey didn't like to break promises. If he agreed to be back at 12.30, he'd be back at 12.30, not a minute before, not a minute later, that was Joey, very precise.

But Joey, though loyal and dependable in many ways, didn't always keep his promises. It wasn't that he meant to break them, it was just that sometimes he got into trouble because of the way he was. He never harmed anyone and believed in what was right, but he was always determined to seek the truth, and this could lead, so Joey believed, to circumstances beyond his control.

His parents had told him about Leo, that he was a long-lost cousin and the 'spitting image' of Kevin. They said he was just visiting Edinburgh and had now gone home to Birmingham.

But Joey had overheard them talking when they came back from meeting him the other night and he'd heard them say Leo was staying at the Minerva Hotel.

Joey had phoned Sean about it and Sean told him Leo had been staying at the Minerva but had to leave because he'd got himself into some kind of trouble with gangsters. Sean warned Joey to stay away and promised to take him to visit Leo sometime in the future.

Joey was riding towards the city centre and decided to check out the Minerva anyway. He thought about gangland Edinburgh. He knew they'd got some of his mates selling drugs and each area was covered and protected by a gang. Basically, these gangsters buy you the best clothes and trainers, make you feel important, teach you respect and loyalty. In return you carry and sell stuff but if you get caught you never give a name. You just say, 'Someone gave me money to do this stuff, they wouldn't tell me their names.' If you spill the beans you get stabbed or shot, it's your own fault for getting caught, you just have to take it. None of them fear the law. Even if you go to prison it's better than the alternative. His mates had tried to get him into it and had offered him free stuff to try but Joey knew there was enough going on in his head already without mind-bending drugs screwing him up further. Unknown to them, he'd watched as they'd worked their beat or as they were picked up or dropped off by a black Range Rover. Rumour had it that they worked for Jake McCullen's gang.

Trial bike mad Joey, helmet and gloves on, pulled a few hops and manuals as he neared the city, with the music of Band of Horses beating through his earphones. The music was a bit old school but what was good for Danny MacAskill was good enough for him. Indeed, it was Danny's video 'Inspired Bicycles' that first got him into learning the tricks and Danny was his hero, a legend.

It was the very soundtrack 'Funeral' from that video that was now playing as Joey saw it … The black Range Rover. He recognised the number plate (probably duplicated) — Joey never forgot numbers. Now for some fun, he thought.

Mattie eased the Range Rover, with his passenger, along the Grassmarket towards

Cowgate. A loud bang startled even Mattie's dull senses as a youth on a bike landed on the Range Rover's bonnet. Mattie hit the brakes but in a second the youth was down and away, pedalling towards the Cowgate roundabout. Mattie pulled away and as he reached the roundabout, the youth came around forcing him to stop, Mattie blasted on the horn and inched towards him. The youth was gesturing at him. Mattie pressed the window winder down and took a pistol out of his pocket.

'Put that fucking thing away!' Arnold shouted. 'Jake said you were stupid, but I didn't think you were that stupid, now let me out and you get the hell out of here, I'll make my own way back.'

The youth took off down Cowgate as Arnold got out and Mattie roared off.

Arnold walked back towards Grassmarket, on past all the old pubs until he came to the last one where he about turned. Making sure the fuss had died down and that no one had noticed him, he retraced his steps, passing the roundabout and continuing along Cowgate. He crossed over and walked past the Minerva Hotel on the opposite side, glancing across as he went.

The foyer was littered with bags and suitcases, and busy with guests checking out. He walked a few metres further then crossed and made his way back before turning in to the side of the hotel and up to the service entrance where he swiped the pass and let himself in.

Joey thought he'd push his luck no further and scooted off down Cowgate, up Blair Street and across to High Street and his favourite descent, Carrubber's Close. With a series of spectacular hops and leaps, he flew down the steps, spinning around at the bottom and speeding off in the direction of Waverley. He chained his bike up at the station and headed back for the Minerva on foot.

Inside the service entrance was a choice of three doors and a stairway to the left, Arnold took the stairs, climbing to the third floor where a sign informed him: 'Rooms 120-140'. He slipped on his black silk gloves and partially opened the door that led to the corridor. He heard another door open so gently eased the stair door back. He waited a while as a couple emerged from the next room up and walked away down the corridor. He opened the door a fraction and watched them as they called the lift. He could see room 120 and room 121 with its 'Do Not Disturb' sign hanging on the door handle. When the couple disappeared into the lift, Arnold made his move.

He swiped his pass in the slot, gently turned the door handle, and waited... no reaction. He pushed the door open a few millimetres, keeping his foot against it and peered in through the tiny gap. The room was dark, save for a chink of light coming from the curtain join. He could see the slot where you insert the room pass to activate the lights. There was no card in it. Strange, he thought. He eased the door open further revealing two boots beside the bed and the shape of a body under the duvet. He stepped into the room, silently closing the door behind him.

Joey climbed the steep steps of Fleshmarket Close, turned left into Cockburn Street, crossed the High Street to Blair Street and made his way back down to Cowgate.

There was no sign of the black Range Rover as he arrived outside the hotel and he wondered where it might have been going. He took a deep breath, opened the huge glass door, and walked up to the reception desk.

Arnold drew the knife from his inside pocket and crept to the edge of the bed. Knife at the ready, he slowly lifted the duvet back to reveal… pillows! Pillows and blankets had been made into the shape of a body. The Ghost of Edinburgh was gone!

The tall, attractive receptionist looked down at Joey.

'What can I do for you, Sonny?'

Joey reddened. 'I'm looking for my uncle.'

'And what's that got to do with the Minerva Hotel?'

'His name's Leo Coyne, I believe he may be staying here.'

'We couldn't possibly disclose our guest list to just anyone walking in off the street,' she said, rather haughtily.

'If he is here, could you just ring his room and tell him his nephew, Joe is here? Please, it's important,' Joey pleaded with her.

'Very well,' her manner softened slightly, 'wait there a moment.'

She tapped into a keyboard, scanned a screen then picked up a phone.

Joey waited for what seemed like an age.

'There's no reply, funny that, he was here last night and was due to check out this morning but hasn't done so yet.'

'Could you get someone to check his room?' Joey asked, 'He could be in danger.'

The receptionist picked up the phone again.

A porter appeared and disappeared into the lift with a nod to the receptionist.

Joey waited while she dealt with more guests checking out.

Eventually the porter appeared at the counter.

'He's gone, he must have done a runner,' the porter said. 'Strange thing is,' the porter continued, 'he left his boots and all the spare pillows and blankets are under the duvet. Perhaps we should call—'

But before the porter could finish that sentence, Joey was gone.

*****

A man with a rucksack on his back and violin case in his hand, and a woman carrying nothing at all, stepped off the tram at Edinburgh Park Station. They crossed to the railway station and boarded an Edinburgh to Glasgow stopping train. They found seats together in the half-empty diesel multiple unit.

Out of earshot of any of the other passengers the woman spoke.

'Look, thanks for doing this, I think you are wonderful, you are my hero.'

'And I think you are the best thing in the world,' the man replied.

'You are very brave taking me with you,' she said, squeezing his hand.

'Brave, why?' the man asked.

'Jake will find us, you know, and when he does, he will kill us.'

'Maybe, maybe not,' the man looked nonplussed.

She looked into his eyes and whispered, 'He knows your name and that you live in Birmingham.'

'Well,' he said, pausing, and looking straight ahead, 'I don't actually live in Birmingham,' he paused again then continued, 'but I suppose he could track us down. We've certainly got some thinking to do. For a start you've got nothing but the clothes you are wearing, no bank cards, nothing!'

'Jake scattered the contents of my bag on the floor of my apartment, but he'll have gone back there. He's probably reported them stolen, faked a burglary or something.'

'He could even have reported you missing to the police,' Jake whispered. 'They could be looking for you right now.'

Fiona was silent.

'It's difficult to know which way Jake will play it, Fiona, we might have to go to the police, you've got enough on him.'

'I can't do that, he's too well in with the top brass. Once Jake knows where I am, I'm a goner.'

Leo decided to change the subject.

'When we get to Glasgow, we'll do a bit of shopping, get you sorted out. Then we'll head south. You'll have to risk hiding out at my place for a while, it's pretty secure. I don't know whether Jake will be able to trace my address. The only place in Edinburgh that will have it is the hotel. Talking of which, I must phone and apologise for not checking out and let them know I'll post my room pass to them.'

'But Leo, I haven't got any money,' Fiona fretted.

'Don't worry about that for now, but the truth is I haven't got an endless bank account and you can't access yours. You are going to have to go to the police sooner or later.'

'I've told you, I can't! You wouldn't believe the connections that guy has got. He does jobs for the police; he's even done stuff for the government.'

For the first time Leo looked worried.

'Now that is scary,' Leo shuddered.

He thought for a while, listening to the rhythm of the train on the tracks and watching the scenery change from rural to urban, through the rain-splattered window.

'We'll have to plan something,' he said eventually, 'perhaps go to Ireland.

*****

Joey strode up Blair Street and soon disappeared among the morning crowds of tourists and shoppers. Back at Waverley, he unchained his bike and cycled home.

'Where have you been?' asked Jean, as Joey entered the kitchen.

'Nowhere.'

'You've been up to something,' she said, while continuing to chop vegetables for a stew she was making.

'No Mam, just been for a ride.'

'Better than being stuck on that PlayStation, I suppose,' she said, as he went through to the hall and up to his room,

Later in the day he phoned his uncle, Sean and told him about what had happened earlier at the Minerva, deliberately omitting to tell him about his bike antics.

'I told you to keep out of this,' Sean answered angrily.

'But you said he'd gone yesterday, and they told me he was there last night.'

'Well he's gone now. Look, I've promised to take you to see him. I'm telling you to keep out of this for your own safety and if you don't listen to me, Joe, I'm going to fall out with you.'

'Ok, ok, I'm sorry uncle,' Joey pleaded. 'I'm sorry.'

*****

Another train, this time Glasgow to London Euston, stopping at among other places, Coventry. Fiona and Leo had seats together and were settled in for the journey. After shopping for clothes and essentials in Glasgow and getting changed and spruced up in the station ladies' room, Fiona was feeling almost human. They were both in better spirits after a hearty lunch at

Waxy O'Connor's and Leo dozed in between reading newspapers while Fiona lost herself in a book she'd bought. They said little and Leo's mind began to wander. It was as though he was looking at himself from across the other side of the train. Is this really me?

Have I really done what I've done, and have I got a clue what I'm going to do next?

'Are you ok?' Fiona broke his reverie.

'Of course, why?'

'You were staring ahead as if in a trance.'

'Oh! I was miles away, I'm ok.' He kissed her and smiled.

The journey passed quietly and a melancholy feeling, that Leo always got when he returned from his travels, came over him as he recognised the lights of Coventry.

They left the train and jumped into a waiting black cab to take them to Leo's flat.

Arriving at the flat, Leo felt slightly embarrassed, remembering that Fiona had lived in a luxury apartment.

'It's probably not up to Meadows standard,' he said as he unlocked the two locks on his sturdy front door, 'but it's got a good shower and bath!'

'It'll be fine.' Fiona replied.

He kicked away a pile of junk mail and a Coventry Observer from behind the door as he flicked the lights on and tapped in the alarm code.

'I'll sort that lot later, let's get a drink. I'm having a dram; I had enough coffee on the train. You?'

'Why not! Water with mine please.'

'Coming up, take a seat.'

Fiona sat on Leo's huge sofa while he fixed the drinks.

He joined her on the sofa, ignoring his favourite armchair.

'Cheers!' he proposed.

'Cheers! Our future!' Fiona replied.

'Whatever that may hold,' Leo continued.

'Talking of which, we won't be safe here for long. Jake is bound to trace us. Tomorrow I want you to write down everything you've got on him. We've got to get someone on our side. A local detective, a solicitor or a newspaper otherwise his secrets die with us!'

Chapter 9

The next morning, Leo woke early. The night before, Fiona, exhausted by the trauma of the previous two days, had fallen asleep straight away, and was still asleep now. She looked a picture of tranquillity, almost child-like and Leo lightly kissed her, but she did not stir.

He left the bedroom, went through to the kitchen and put the kettle on. Realising he had no milk, he decided to pop out to the corner shop. Noticing the pile of junk mail by the door, he sorted out the few letters that were for him, put them aside and took the rest down with him to throw in the recycling bin.

Fiona woke to the clunk of the closing door and for a few seconds wondered where the hell she was. The events of the previous days eventually ran through her mind and she slowly got out of bed.

In the kitchen she discovered two mugs and a teapot on the table. She felt the kettle; it was hot but there was no sign of Leo.

The little kitchen had a dining table and a couple of chairs, there wasn't room for much else. She decided to acquaint herself with the rest of the flat as she hadn't taken much notice of anything the night before. It was a typical 1960's-built place but Leo had got it quite tastefully done out. The living room was half-study, half-lounge, with a collection of books, records, CDs, tapes and musical instruments crammed into the study area. A desk with a lap-top completed the scene. The lounge half was tidy and minimalistic with a sofa, armchair, coffee table, TV and hi-fi and a couple of paintings of mountain views.

She gave the bathroom a quick once-over then decided to take a shower.

Leo returned with bread, milk and a few other odds and ends. He could hear the shower running and shouted through.

'Cup of tea?'

'Yes please,' she shouted back, above the din of the shower.

She eventually appeared in the kitchen, dressed simply in jeans and a new T-shirt that she'd bought the day before.

She pecked him on the cheek and joined him at the table.

'I'm afraid I can only offer you cereals and toast at the moment,' he told her.

'That's fine,' she replied'

'When I've finished my tea. I'm going to walk to the supermarket to do a food shop. I've very little in because of being away, and the corner shop doesn't stock much. We can have a proper breakfast when I get back if you like.'

'That sounds good, I'm starving,'

Leo drank the last of his tea.

'Look, I'm going to go now, just help yourself to anything you want, I won't be long but there's one thing I want you to do.'

He took out a notebook and pen and pushed them across the table.

'I want you to write down everything you've got on Jake; drugs, prostitution, money laundering, protection rackets, the lot.'

'I'm not sure I want to do that. I'm scared!'

'Fiona, the information is going nowhere for now, just make a few notes for me, please!'

Leo stood up, flung his empty rucksack over his shoulder and put his hand on Fiona's arm.

'Bye now, see you soon,' he said and left the flat.

Fiona helped herself to cereal and then made another cup of tea. She found Leo's tobacco and rolled a cigarette.

Then she started writing.

After half an hour she stopped and read it through.

Her hands were shaking. She poured herself a glass of water, rolled another cigarette and read it through again. Then she put the notebook away in a drawer.

She went to the study area and looked at his collection of books. There were guidebooks on walking in Ireland and Scotland, song books, music tutors and all manner of novels. She picked books out randomly and flicked through them. She studied his CD collection and then came upon a Toby jug containing a collection of tin whistles. She took out one of them. She hadn't played one of these since she'd left school. She started to play but could not get the notes to sound right, especially the higher range, but gradually the technique started to come back to her.

Leo, with a rucksack full of groceries, opened the front door. He could hear a rudimentary version of Fáinne *Geal an Lae* (*The Dawning of the Day*) being played on a tin whistle. He quietly placed the rucksack on the floor and did not shut the door. He tip-toed into the lounge, Fiona had her back to him, and he stood and listened. When she had finished, he applauded.

She spun round.

'Oh! Leo it's you, you frightened me,' she said, looking slightly embarrassed.

'That was lovely. I sing *Raglan Road* to that tune. You can accompany me.'

'You seem to have a song for every situation.'

'Well, Liam Clancy once said, 'Songs are like ghosts, out there in the ether, waiting…''

'That's very profound, who's Liam Clancy?'

'You are Irish, and you've never heard of the Clancy Brothers of Aran sweater fame?'

'Oh! Yes, my dad used to have one of their L.P.s.'

Leo went back to close the front door and brought the rucksack in.

He walked over to the jug of whistles.

'I sing it in C,' he said, taking a whistle out of the jug.

'Here's a C whistle, it's the same fingering as the D, try it.

He took his fiddle out and played the opening line. Fiona joined in and they played it through together, then he sang the verses with just the whistle for accompaniment.

'Great!' he said, when they had finished.

'Now for a late breakfast, we'll call it brunch.'

He went into the kitchen and re-stocked the fridge and larder, then set to work preparing brunch.

'Need any help?' Fiona asked him.

'No, I'm fine, I'm used to cooking, albeit usually for one.'

'Here,' he gave her a newspaper, 'go and relax, I'll call you when it's ready.'

Over, brunch, Leo said, 'There's a session at the Irish Club on a Sunday afternoon, we could go there, if you like. It's mainly old boys and you are as likely to hear *Take me Home, Country Roads* as you are an Irish reel. They have piano accordion and pass the mic round but it's ok and I know the barman and a few of the crowd. What do you think?'

'Your call, Leo, so long as I won't feel out of place.'

'You'll be fine, I'll take the fiddle and you can take the whistle.'

'Oh, I don't know about that!'

Brunch being over, they had another cup of tea and Fiona knew what was coming next.

'Did you manage to write anything down?' Leo asked her.

Fiona walked to the drawer, took out the notebook and placed it in front of Leo, without saying a word.

Leo opened it and started reading.

Jake McCullen owns a string of legitimate businesses in Edinburgh and Central Scotland including the one where I work. There are motor sales companies and car hire franchises, taxi companies, shops, take-aways, nightclubs, bars, and restaurants. Also, he owns property letting, estate agents and loan companies. This empire, I believe, was founded and funded on the proceeds of organised crime. This includes drug dealing, prostitution, protection rackets. people smuggling and slavery. His organization is bringing in refugees who have paid big money to get here. They are living above take-aways, in attics and warehouses where they are put to work. They are too frightened to go to the police as they are illegals and know they will probably be deported if they do.

Jake's latest line of business is supplying guns and ammunition. He gets away with all of this because he also provides 'services' to politicians, police chiefs. judges, and the like. And he has them all in his pocket.

'Phew! There's plenty to go on there,' Leo said, closing the notebook.

'What I don't understand,' he continued, 'is, if Jake has all these legitimate businesses, why does he bother, or take the risks with crime anymore?'

'Ego,' Fiona said. 'If you knew Jake, you'd know he has to be the big boss; he has to control Edinburgh, he has to be the king of Edinburgh!'

'I see. Is there anyone you could phone to see what's going on now?'

'Too risky, and I can only remember a few numbers. Jake will have my phone and will have rung all of my contacts to see if any of them know of my whereabouts.'

'Shit! I've just thought, my number will be on your phone.' Leo looked alarmed.

'Don't worry,' she reassured him, 'I have a way of memorising your number and I deleted after every call.'

'I thought I'd never see you again, you know.'

'Why?'

'After that first night, I found the note with my number on it, screwed up in a ball in the bin.'

'Good job I've got a good memory!' Fiona beamed.

'What about your parents?'

'What about them?'

'Is their number on your phone?'

'Yes, their number is on my phone. I told Marie at the shop that I had to go away to a family funeral. Now Jake will have got that out of her and may have contacted my parents.'

Fiona was thinking aloud; 'I know their number. I'll send them a text to let them know I'm ok, if you lend me your phone. They'll know it's me because I'll use the nickname they had for me when I was a child.'

'Oh yea, what is it?' Leo asked, with a grin.

'Ricky,' Fiona replied, looking slightly embarrassed.

'That's all right, it suits you. But why Ricky?'

'When I was a kid my hair was like a hayrick, now lend me your phone!'

Leo handed her the phone and she thumbed in the number. It was one she could remember.

Hello Mam, just a quick text as I've lost my phone and am using someone else's. Just to let you know I'm ok. I will be in touch in a day or so. Lots of love Ricky xxx.

She handed it back to Leo and he pocketed it.

Minutes later it beeped. Leo read the message. 'Looks like Jake's on to us,' he said as he handed the phone back to Fiona.

She read the text:

Hello Darling, we've been worried about you. Some feller with a scotch accent phoned last night asking if we knew where you were. When I said Edinburgh, he just rang off, number withheld. I tried phoning you, please keep in touch. Love M.

Fiona texted the reply:

Don't worry, will speak to you as soon as I get my phone sorted. Love R x.

She handed the phone back to Leo.

'Jake is busy this weekend, he has a couple of really big deals to oversee but when it's over, he'll concentrate on finding me. And when he does, after my escape from the warehouse and what he thinks I did to Crina, he'll either kill me or promote me.'

'Perhaps we'd better think about moving somewhere else for a while,' Leo said, 'I have a friend who lives in the wilds of East Clare, in a big old farmhouse. I'm sure he'd let us stay if I explained our predicament. We could lie low there for a while. I might give him a call later. Anyway look, let's forget about it for now and go and relax at the club for a couple of hours.'

'Ok,' Fiona replied, 'Can I use your laptop before we go?'

'Of course, any reason?'

'I just want to check the Edinburgh news.'

'Ok, that's fine.'

Leo went to the laptop and logged on.

'There you are.'

Leo washed up and tidied the kitchen while Fiona got on the laptop. She checked the websites of The Edinburgh News and The Edinburgh Reporter and even The Daily Record and The Scotsman.

'Doesn't look like Jake's gone public about me going missing,' she said to Leo, when he rejoined her.

'Mind you, Jake has his own way of doing things,' she added.

'Right, I'll phone a taxi if you're ready,' Leo changed the subject.

He booked a cab and got his things together, picking up the C and D whistles, 'Mustn't forget these,' he said with a grin.

'Look Leo, I haven't played since I was at school.'

'Don't worry, you've only got to play one tune and you've rehearsed that.'

'I'd rather not,' Fiona pleaded.

The taxi dropped them of at The Irish Club and Leo paid the fare.

The club, set among industrial units, was built in the 1950's and was now showing signs of age and looking rather shabby, although it boasted a proper dance floor with many a stiletto heel print pock-marking its polished wooden surface.

The dance room was not in use today, so they went through to the lounge area where the music session was already in progress. Leo put his fiddle case down and motioned Fiona to seats at a table to the side of where the musicians were playing.

'What'll you have? I'm having Guinness,' Leo whispered.

'I'll have the same, thanks,' Fiona replied and sat down while Leo went to the bar.

'Hello Leo, how are you?' the man behind the bar asked.

'I'm fine, Brendan, you're looking well as usual.'

Brendan, the club steward, was a larger than life Kerry man with huge hands and a huge smile.

'Can't complain. I didn't see you Friday night?'

'No, I've been away.'

'Anyway, what are you having?'

'Two Guinness please.'

'Coming up, who is the dame?'

Oh, that's Ricky, a friend. She's from Donegal originally.'

'Batting above your average, aren't you?'

'Whadya mean?' Leo snapped in mock indignation.'

Brendan winked and continued pouring the Guinness.

Back at the table, during a lull in the music, Leo introduced Fiona as Ricky to the musicians and she glared at him while smiling politely at the others.

Sheedy, the bodhran player, no one knew his first name, he was known as Oul' Sheedy or just Sheedy, stood up and insisted on kissing her. A jaunty fellow in a tweed jacket, he had a collection of spoons and bones and was accompanied by a small terrier whom he promised would dance for her later.

Then there was Pat, a small fellow with a bald head, behind a piano accordion, his head just peeping above it. What is it with accordion players? Leo thought, they all seem to be small guys hidden behind their instruments! The piano accordion seemed to be popular here and in Scotland but not in Ireland where the smaller button melodeons were used. A musician in Ireland once told Leo that they didn't like accordion players in sessions because they played between the cracks!

Pat was also a fine singer and a tough little fellow who had served in the Irish Army Peacekeeping Force in the Sinai Desert. *Peace Enforcers*, he called them.

Next to Pat was his wife, Mary, smartly dressed and handsome for her age. She played rudimentary fiddle, in strict time, as she did when playing for the Irish Dancing classes.

Completing the group was Fergus, a tall thin man with a shock of grey hair, who played flute and tin whistle.

These people were older than Leo and had, like a lot of other club members, with the exception of Pat and Mary, come over to England during the 1960's to work on the roads and the building sites.

Some had done well and started up their own businesses, but they'd all had hard lives and you could see it in their faces and their hands.

The merriment went on and Leo went to the bar for a second round. He ordered the drinks and quietly asked Brendan, 'Do you get any CID in here?'

'It's not like the old days you know,' Brendan said, looking puzzled, 'why do you ask?'

'Oh, I just thought you might keep in with them and maybe have a contact.'

'You in some kind of trouble?'

'Could be. I need someone I could have a discreet word with, off the record, if you know what I mean.'

Brendan contemplated him for a while, then said, 'Give me your phone number, I'll see what I can do.'

Leo thanked him, returned with the drinks, and took out his fiddle to join in.

The afternoon continued and a more relaxed Fiona duly played her whistle tune with Leo easing off to allow her a solo, which drew a round of applause and calls for more. The group had a radio microphone which transmitted to a speaker that was placed on a nearby table, Various members of the audience came up and did songs and Leo's prediction came true when a woman came up and asked, 'Can you play *Take Me Home Country Roads*?'

*****

At about the time the taxi had dropped Leo and Fiona off at the club, Joey was cycling through Leith. He'd been for a ride around Ocean Terminal and the docks, and stopping at the Bernard street traffic lights, he spotted a familiar sight ahead. The black Range Rover parked in the lay-by on the bridge. He dismounted, lifted the bike onto the pavement and stood by the closed side door of the King's Wark pub. The traffic lights changed, and a large white Sprinter type van pulled up behind the Range Rover. Joey watched as a tall man with long, fair hair emerged from the passenger side of the Rover, walked round to the driver's side of the van and spoke to the driver for a few minutes. He then returned to the Rover which pulled away followed by the van. Joey got back on his bike and also followed, keeping his distance.

The two vehicles turned left and made their way through to Ferry Road, then took another left into an area of warehouses.

There was a fair amount of traffic for a Sunday, enabling him to keep up with them without getting too close, but now he had to be careful because these backstreets were almost deserted.

He held back at each corner and waited for them to turn before making a move. He thought he'd lost them when he turned into an empty street but heard the clanking of metal gates ahead. He got off his bike and kept well in by the wall of an old warehouse. A huge hulk of a man fed a chain through the gates and padlocked it. Joey waited a few minutes, then got back on his bike and sped past the gates. Glancing to his right, he saw the Range Rover among a few other cars in the yard, but there was no sign of the van. He carried on to the side, where railings separated him from the warehouse. There was a door halfway up the back of the building, with a platform and old fire escape steps which were broken and had become partly detached. Joey chained his bike to the railings, clambered over them and hauled himself up onto the platform. He tried the door, but it was locked. To the side, there was a drainpipe which led up to a vee in the roof. He climbed this and edged his way, quietly, like a snake, along the roof. Every now and then there were corrugated Perspex skylights, but they were opaque with age and impossible to see through. He carried on to the other end of the building where one of the skylights was broken. Lying down with his head at the edge of the skylight, he peered through the gap.

Below him a van was being unloaded, Wooden cases were carried from the van and placed carefully on the floor. Then two men prized open one of the cases. The tall man with long fair hair whom he'd seen earlier, took out a pistol from the case and placed it on a sheet of cloth that was spread over a table. Then another case was opened, it was full of rifles. The tall man picked one up, inspected it and placed it with the pistol. Joey reached for his mobile phone and took a photograph through the gap.

Next the two men prized open a larger case and removed a lot of packing material, then the tall man carefully lifted out what looked to Joey like a machine gun.

Joey took another photo and edged away from the skylight. He slithered back along the roof the way he came and in no time was down the drainpipe, off the platform and over the railings.

He unlocked his bike, got his earphones out of his pocket, connected them to his phone and, to the sound of The Prodigy's *Firestarter*, was on his way as fast as he could go. Destination, St Leonards Police Station.

'This'll get me in their good books,' he said to himself.

Joey chained his bike to the railings in St Leonards Lane, checked the photos on his phone, then crossed the road and entered the police station.

'Joseph Anderson!' The desk sergeant raised his eyebrows, 'I don't believe it, we usually have to drag you in here. Have you come to own up to something? Conscience got the better of you?'

'No Sir, I've come to help you.'

'The best way you can help us is by staying off our streets.'

Joey ignored the sergeant's remark, scrolled to the first photo, and slid his phone across the counter without saying a word.

'Jeez! Heckler and Koch assault rifles, loads of them.' The sergeant couldn't help but talk out loud.

But it was when he scrolled to the next photo that he was more shocked.

He let out a low whistle, 'A Point-Fifty calibre high power sniper rifle! That could immobilise a truck from a mile away, where did you get these photos?'

'I've just taken them.'

'Where?' The sergeant looked incredulous.

'A warehouse in Leith,' Joey replied, matter-of-factly.

'Wait there, young man, we'll need to talk to you, you could be in for a big reward,' the Sergeant told him, then garbled a message into the phone.

A woman with a blonde bob, dressed in a smart grey trouser suit and an older man in a crumpled blue suit appeared from a side door. The sergeant passed the phone over the counter to the man, and the woman approached Joey.

'Joseph, I'm Detective Inspector Barnhurst and this is Detective Superintendent Caldwell. Would you like to come through?

'Ok,' Joey replied and followed them through to a well-appointed office, a bit different to the bare interview rooms that he had experienced previously.

'Take a seat Joseph, would you like a drink? Tea, coffee? DI Barnhurst asked him.'

Have you got Irn-Bru? Joey flashed a cheeky smile.

She grinned, 'I'll see what I can do.'

'How about you Peter?' She asked the DS.

'No, I'm fine thanks.'

DI Barnhurst disappeared and the Super, sat behind a desk, with some notes and a lap-top in front of him, spoke to Joey.

'So, you say you've just taken these photos?'

'Yes,' replied Joey, 'in a warehouse in Leith,'

'So how did you get these views from above?'

'I climbed on the roof and took them through a broken skylight.'

'Climbed on the roof?' The DS looked at Joey suspiciously.

'It's what I do,' Joey said, looking into his lap,

'Like climbing into cemeteries after dark,' the DS said, looking at his notes.

Joey gave him a sheepish look but said nothing.

At that point DI Barnhurst returned with a can of Irn-Bru, a paper cup and a coffee. She passed the can and paper cup to Joey.'

'Think yourself lucky, I had to cadge that of a colleague.'

DS Caldwell switched on the laptop and got a map of Edinburgh on the screen.

'Can you tell us exactly where you say you've taken these photos.' He asked Joey.

'Yes, just off Ferry Road.'

Joey pointed to the street where the warehouse is located, and the DS switched to satellite view.

'There it is.' Joey showed him the yard and the side where he had climbed on the roof.

'How long ago did you take these photos?' The DS asked Joey.

'Just now, about twenty minutes ago.'

'Right,' Caldwell said to DI Barnhurst, 'could you come outside for a moment?'

They both left the room, leaving Joey alone.

Once outside the room, Caldwell said to DI Barnhurst, 'Keep him happy, take a statement but don't release him yet, I don't want him getting involved any further, I need to launch an operation urgently!'

DI Barnhurst returned to Caldwell's office and spoke to Joey, 'You've been extremely helpful to us, Joseph, but I'll need to take a statement from you, if that's alright.'

'Am I in trouble?' Joey looked worried.

'No, not at all,' she reassured him, 'we just need a few details.'

'Ok then,' he agreed.

'Oh, by the way, I've left my bike outside,' he added.

'Where is it?'

'It's chained to the railings in St Leonards Lane.'

'Well it should be safe enough, chained to railings outside a police station and there's CCTV everywhere out there but you know Edinburgh! Give me the key and I'll get someone to bring it in.'

'It's a combination.'

He told her the number and she wrote it down.

'Are you expected home?' She asked him.

'In about an hour or so.'

'This may take a while, so I'd better phone your parents and let them know where you are,'

'Tell them I'm not in trouble!' Joey pleaded.

'Don't worry, I will.'

She picked up the phone to arrange for someone to bring Joey's bike in, then phoned Joey's home number.

After a brief conversation, she put the phone down and turned to Joey.

'Ok, I've spoken to your mother and she's coming to the station,'

Joey looked worried.

'Don't worry. I've assured her that you are not in any trouble.' Joey looked unconvinced but did not say anything.

'Now. Shall we get this statement done?'

'If you like,' Joey said, quietly.

'Ok, start from the beginning.'

Joey explained about going for a ride and following the vehicles.

'So, what made you follow these vehicles?' she asked him.

'I recognised the Range Rover,' he decided not to mention his antics in Grassmarket and continued, 'it's one of the cars that picks up boys on our estate and takes them drug dealing.'

'Oh yes?' Barnhurst raised her eyebrows.

'Some lads I know have tried to get me doing it, but no way am I interested in doing that.'

'How can you be sure it was the same Range Rover?'

'I'm good with numbers, I can remember the registration.'

'Really! What is it?'

Joey reeled off the number and DI Barnhurst tapped it into the laptop. Sure enough. The number was a black Range Rover registered keeper, Lindean Limos. She did a check to find they were a used car sales and prestige car hire company based on the edge of the city.

'I don't suppose you can remember the van's number?' She asked him.

'No, I didn't make a mental note of it, but it was unusual, the letters and numbers were in a different order to normal, oh! and it had Z in it.'

'What colour were the plates?'

'I only saw the back one and that was yellow.'

'Joseph, this is particularly useful information, just have a break for a minute while I make a call.'

Joey drank from the can, ignoring the paper cup while DI Barnhurst relayed the information that Joey had provided to DS Caldwell, adding that the van was probably Northern Ireland registered.

She then continued with the statement, getting Joey to give descriptions of the men as best he could.

The description of a tall fair-haired man had a familiarity about it, and she had a suspicion of whom they might be dealing with but kept it to herself.

When the statement was complete, she got Joey to read through it and sign it. She thanked Joey once again, adding, 'You know something, Joseph, I don't think you are a bad lad after all!'

She continued chatting to him, asking if he had ever had a job.

'I've been on a few training schemes and things but when I've applied for a proper job, once they find out I've been to a special school, they don't want to know.'

'That's not fair, Joseph.'

'I know, but my problem is I listen to other people too much, but they should listen to me.'

'How do you mean?'

'Well, for instance, I started having driving lessons, thinking I might get a job if I could drive, but the instructor lost his temper with me.'

'Why was that?'

'I was driving along, and he told me to go straight over the roundabout ...'

Barnhurst bit her lip to suppress a snigger, Joey noticed and stopped talking.

Barnhurst composed herself, 'Sorry Joseph, what did you do?'

'Well, I did what he said and drove straight over it. I thought he was testing me to see if I could do it in case of an emergency or if the road was blocked or something. Anyway, he wouldn't take me again.'

*****

DS Caldwell decided an immediate police operational deployment was necessary and he being the person with ready access to information, communications and resources, took initial command. He put Operations Room Supervisor, Superintendent Anne Bridges, in command at the station while he took charge of the operation on the ground.

Authorised Firearms Officers were called in, Specialist Firearms Units mustered and even the one and only Air Support Unit was requested.

The Police set up roadblocks either end of Ferry Road, cleared all the traffic and sealed off all the adjoining streets.

Fire and Ambulance services were put on emergency alert as Caldwell and his officers moved in on the warehouse.

They surrounded the site and deployed police marksmen in strategic positions. They had investigated the situation as best they could from the outside and had contained the area around the subject. Now it was time to communicate with the subject.

The Range Rover Joey had described was in the yard among other vehicles, behind gates that were chained and padlocked. Caldwell's officers easily cut through the chain, entered the yard and approached the roller shutter doors.

Meanwhile inside the warehouse, Jake and his accomplices had inspected and photographed their delivery and were in the process of re-packing and storing the weaponry.

Jake was alerted by the sound of the lock on the door to the side of the roller door being tampered with, He whispered to his men to take cover. They watched as the door opened a few inches then closed again.

Several police officers protected by shields, then entered and took up position behind the row of packing cases nearest the door.

All was quiet for a few minutes until a loudhailer announcement rang out.

'Notice to all occupants, this building is subject to a police investigation and is surrounded by armed officers. For your own safety, will all occupants please come forward towards the entrance, with your hands above your heads.'

There was a brief period of silence until a loud drumming sound started up. It was the refugees, locked in the portacabins, kicking the walls frantically.

Covered by the din, Jake crept away and phoned his contact at the top of Police Scotland. The conversation ended with 'Call your monkeys off, or your use of my services goes public and you are finished.'

But Jake knew it was probably too late. He also knew he must not be found here.

He crawled back to where Mattie and the other lads were taking cover. The van driver was with them and wanted to give himself up, but Jake instructed them, 'Hold them off, we've got enough weapons, I'll get us out of this somehow.'

The van driver looked at Jake incredulously, 'Are you crazy?'

'Do as I say, or you'll be the first to get it,' Jake told him, through gritted teeth.

The drumming grew louder, and a police officer emerged holding a shield. Mattie fired and the officer dodged back behind a packing case. The police returned fire and Mattie just kept firing back in their general direction.

While all this was going on, Jake slipped away to the fire escape near to where Fiona had been kept captive. He crept up the steps, took the key from the box on the wall and unlocked the door. He turned and fired his pistol at the ammunition cases. There was a tremendous explosion and Mattie's huge body was tossed through the air like a rag doll. He opened the door and stepped out, pistol at the ready, onto the ledge.

A voice called out from a loudhailer in a police van parked behind the railings, 'Drop your weapon and hands in the air, we've got you covered.'

Jake fired in the van's direction, leapt to the ground, and made a run for it.

The police marksman easily picked him off. Jake tripped just before the bullet, aimed for the legs, went straight through his back.

The building was now ablaze, one police officer was injured but the others managed to drag him out as they all left the warehouse by the way they had entered.

DS Caldwell got a message on his radio from his superiors instructing him and his men not to enter the building.

'Too late for that Sir, the place is now ablaze and there are people in there,' he replied.

Several explosions followed.

'It's going off like a firework factory here,' he continued, 'We need as many fire appliances down here as possible and get the Fire Service Incident Commander to contact me at the gate.'

An ambulance was sent through the gates and the injured officer, who had been hit in the leg by one of Mattie's random shots was taken care of. The ambulance sped off and DS Caldwell and the remaining officers withdrew to the gates.

The Fire Incident Commander located Caldwell, who informed him that he thought there could still be people alive in there.

'There are several portacabins on the opposite side to where we entered, which would mean they are this side of the building. We heard loud drumming and could see vague shapes through the meshed windows. I think there could be people locked up in there.'

'Ok, we'll assess the situation, but it looks extremely dangerous,' the Commander replied.

The area around the roller door was now ablaze and the roof had fallen in, the flames lighting up the darkening Leith sky.

The firefighters found an old boarded up entrance on the opposite side of the warehouse and despite fears of increasing the draught, they decided to give it a go.

They broke down part of the old entrance and firefighters with breathing apparatus entered the building.

Extra ambulances were called and ready, and after what seemed like an age the fire fighters emerged with two men and five women crawling on their hands and knees. They were taken to the waiting ambulances. One of the men was screaming in broken English, 'More, more, there are more of us … next … next door!'

The firefighters re-entered the building but despite the best efforts of the Aerial Ladder Platforms (ALPs) and Turntable Ladder Appliances (TTLs) pumping 2.400 litres of water per minute each, the fire had spread. The hundreds of wooden packing cases and pallets making ideal fuel.

They had no choice but to quickly retreat but they could see that all that was left of the portacabins were grim burnt out frames.

Anyone left in there would not have stood a chance.

Chapter 10

Fiona was up and about early but Leo was still fast asleep. The session had gone on quite late and they'd had a takeaway on the way home. She decided not to disturb him, made a cup of tea and logged on to the laptop. Leo had a BBC shortcut on the screen. She clicked on it and the news page came up. The headline jumped out at her,

POLICE OFFICER INJURED IN SHOOT-OUT AND EXPLOSION AT EDINBURGH WAREHOUSE. ONE DEAD, MORE FATALITIES FEARED.

She read on.

One police officer has been wounded and at least one person killed in a shoot-out followed by fire and explosions at a warehouse in the Leith district of Edinburgh.

It is not known how many people were in the building, but it is believed, but not confirmed, that several gunmen were killed in the explosions.

Firefighters have rescued seven people believed to be refugees.

Witnesses report hearing several explosions and it took the Fire Services until the early hours of this morning to bring the blaze under control.

Police have stated that until investigations are carried out, they can neither confirm nor deny that they are treating the incident as terror related.

Fiona looked at the photo that accompanied the news article but the view of the charred remains of the warehouse could have been anywhere. But she knew, she just knew, this was the place where she had been kept captive.

She darted through to the bedroom and woke Leo.

'Leo, look at this!'

A groggy Leo rubbed his eyes, 'Bloody hell! Is it Jake's warehouse?'

'It has to be.'

Leo jumped out of bed, showered and dressed.

'I'm phoning Edinburgh before I do anything else,' he told Fiona, who was busy in the lounge, searching through the Scottish TV and newspaper websites.

He went into the kitchen and called Sean.

'Hello, Sean? It's Leo. I'm back home —'

'Good!' Sean interrupted.

'I've got Fiona with me,' Leo continued.

'You're crazy! Sean paused then added, 'but you might not have to worry about Jake anymore. It's not official but the word is out that Jake was killed in the shoot-out at the warehouse last night.'

'Really?' Leo said

'That's what I'm hearing. There'll be some jostling for control but most of his cronies will keep a low profile or just disappear while the investigation is carried out. Other gangs could move in, I'm glad I'm well out of it.'

Leo wondered where all this would leave Fiona.

'Are you still there?' Sean asked.

'Yes, sorry I—'

Sean cut him short, 'Leo, can I trust you to keep a secret?'

'Yes. Of course.'

'Well you might not believe this, but young Joey tipped the police off about the warehouse. I don't want you to breathe his name to anyone, understood?'

'You have my word, but how did Joey know about it?'

'Don't ask, look, we'll all meet up when this has blown over but if I were you, I'd get Fiona to go to the police. If she co-operates, they might go easy on her.'

'That's what I was thinking. I'll be in touch, take care Sean.'

'And you take care, Leo.'

Leo walked back into the lounge.

'Looks like you won't have to worry about Jake anymore,' he said to Fiona.

'What!'

'He's been killed in the shoot-out by all accounts.'

'There's nothing about that in the news, how come you know so much?'

'Look, I'm hungry, let's get breakfast and I'll explain.'

Over breakfast, Leo told Fiona all about his newly discovered family in Edinburgh.

'That was my cousin I was speaking to just now.'
He went on to explain how people were doing a
double take on him, standing and staring as he
walked past them. How he met his cousins and
discovered he was the spitting image of their
brother, Kevin, who had died a year previously.
'People thought I was his ghost!'
'So, you are the ghost from the Ghost Town,'
Fiona grinned.
'What?'
'The Specials, *Ghost Town*. Coventry is their town
isn't it?'
'Oh, I see what you mean, but that song could
have been about any town, according to Jerry
Dammers, the guy who wrote it. Mind you it
didn't go down well with all Coventry residents.
A lot of them resented their city being
characterised as a town in decline, but we're
going off the subject now.'
'Anyway,' Leo resumed, 'my cousin used to be
involved in the action, if you know what I mean,
he's done time, a reformed character now but he
still has his contacts. He says the word is out ...
Jake's been killed.'
'I'd rather know for definite,' Fiona said, looking
far from convinced.
'He also says the best thing you could do would
be to co-operate with the police, help them with
their enquiries. He reckons they'd go easy on
you, even grant you immunity from
prosecution.'

'I'd need to be sure about Jake before I did that and anyway, I haven't broken the law, I had a legitimate job.'

'Well, you've got to sort your affairs out. There's your job, your car, the apartment, possessions and bank accounts.'

'Yes, I know but I don't know what to do for the best.'

'Fiona, I've got a confession to make, I spoke to Brendan, the steward at the club, yesterday. I asked him if he'd got any contacts in the local CID, someone to have a quiet word with, off the record. He's going to see what he can do. He's taken my number to pass on.'

As if on cue, Leo's phone rang.

'Hello.' Leo answered.

'Hello, is that Leo Coyne?'

'Yes.'

'I'm Detective Inspector Alison Boyle, I understand you wanted to speak to someone in confidence?'

'Well yes, me and the person who's here with me.'

'Can I ask what it is concerning?'

Leo thought quickly.

'I believe we may have information regarding yesterday's shoot-out in Edinburgh.'

'I see, is it ok to come around now?'

'Just a moment,' Leo shielded the phone.

'Fiona, it's Inspector Alison Boyle, she can come here now. Will you talk to her?'

'Err, I don't know.' Fiona looked worried.

'Look it's in confidence,' Leo assured her.

'Well alright then,' she replied, reluctantly.'

'Hello.' Leo resumed the telephone conversation. 'Yes, you can come now if you like.'

Leo gave her the address and ten minutes later she was at the door.

She was in her late thirties, dark haired and athletically built.

Leo invited her in and offered her a seat, 'Tea, coffee?'

'No thanks, I'll get straight down to business if that's ok with you.'

'That's fine,' Leo replied, 'This is Fiona, she lives in Edinburgh.'

'Hi Fiona, I'm Detective Inspector Alison Boyle, but just call me Alison,' the DI said, sensing she could be on to something big here and aiming to put Fiona at ease.

'Before we start I must warn you that although I will be as discreet as I can with whatever information you give me, if I believe that you or anyone else is in danger, I may have to report the matter.'

'The problem,' Fiona interjected, 'is that I believe I am putting my life in danger by talking to you.'

'Sorry if I sounded a bit officious.' the DI tried to reassure her, 'Look it's ok, this is a confidential chat, it will be up to you if you wish to make a statement. Why don't we take it one step at a time?'

Fiona looked across at Leo.

'Why don't you show Alison the notes,' he suggested.

'Do you think I should?'

'Why not, it'll save a lot of explaining.'

Fiona got up, went to the kitchen, and took the notebook out of the drawer. She returned and handed it, open paged, to Alison.

The DI read it through twice.

'These are pretty serious allegations, Fiona.'

'That is why I was afraid to tell you. Jake abducted me from my apartment, held me captive in that warehouse and threatened to kill me.'

'So how come you're here in Coventry?'

'I escaped and am hiding out here. Leo is helping me out. I have nothing, all my possessions, my phone, my bank cards, they are all in the apartment, which is owned by Jake's organisation, by the way.'

'And you chose not to go to the police in Edinburgh?'

'Afraid to, Jake's too well connected.'

'I would advise you to come and make a statement with us. The police will give you full protection if what you are saying is true.'

Leo, who had been listening quietly spoke, 'I have reason to believe that Jake McCullen was killed in yesterday's shoot-out.'

'If Jake's been killed, Fiona continued, 'I'm willing to co-operate with the police, if he's alive, I'm still afraid.'

'I'm obviously not familiar with this case as it's a different force,' the DI stated.

'Could you just find out about Jake McCullen?' Leo asked, 'And get back to us, we're not going to run away. If it's true, Fiona goes with you, if it's not true, it's up to you to persuade her.'

'I'll see what I can do, I'll need to take your details before I can continue with this.'

DI Boyle took the details and left.

Later that day she returned with the unofficial confirmation that Jake McCullen was dead, Fiona accompanied her to the station where she made a statement and agreed to return to Edinburgh.

Back in Edinburgh, Fiona was taken by the police to her apartment where they forced entry. Everything was as it was left when Jake had abducted her. The only thing that was missing was her phone and this was later recovered from Jakes's property although the police held on to it as evidence. Fiona was helping the police untangle an extremely complicated web as best she could on a daily basis. She decided it was best to move out of the apartment and relocated to a rented flat in the Stockbridge area of Edinburgh. Once settled in, she invited Leo to join her.

Leo had been kicking his heels on the streets of the Ghost Town for a week now, with only the daily phone calls from Fiona on her new phone, to sustain him. But now he was preparing to return to Edinburgh, and he had a celebration to plan. He'd been to the club the day before where his musician friends had enthusiastically agreed to a weekend in Edinburgh. He'd checked dates with Sean and family and got Fiona to phone around her friends.

Back in Edinburgh, this time with a large suitcase instead of a rucksack, he'd sought out Fiona's new apartment and reunited with her. He was glad to be with her again and she'd welcomed him unconditionally, but it all seemed unreal.

He felt uncertain about the future and decided he needed to discuss it with her.

After he'd cooked dinner the following evening and they were sat together, finishing off a bottle of wine, he decided to broach the subject.

'Fiona, I'd just like to say that it's fantastic being here with you and this is a fabulous place to live, it's just that I feel a bit unsure about the future.'

'That's understandable, Leo, she replied, 'but you want to live in Edinburgh, and I want you here with me, so let's just see how it goes for a while. Just enjoy it.'

'That's very kind of you, I'm just worried that although we've been through a lot together, we haven't known each other all that long.'

'Look, I've got a lot to sort out before I can start thinking about my future. You can keep hold of your flat in Coventry, perhaps even rent it out, and we'll see where we are when the police are finished with me.'

Leo took her hand. 'I didn't mean to trouble you Fiona, I'm really happy here with you.'

'You relax and go and organise your party.' She smiled and kissed him.

Now ensconced in Edinburgh, Leo dropped into Sandy Bell's on a quiet weekday afternoon. After ordering a pint he enquired of the landlord,

'Excuse me, I'm planning a small celebration and wondered if we would be ok to hold it here. I'm looking at a Saturday afternoon, there'd be fifteen to twenty of us, some musician friends of nine, old Irish guys, up from the midlands, and a few locals.'

'The musicians will be fine, not sure about the locals though,' the landlord replied, fixing Leo with a steely glare.

'No?'

The landlord's face cracked, 'Only joking! We don't encourage stags or the like, but we have had rugby teams and rapper dancers in. Ye'll be fine but we do have a session going about two o'clock. Your friends would be welcome to join in if they know the crack. You play yourself, don't you?'

'Yes, I play a bit of fiddle.'

'I thought I recognised you, you'll know the score then.'

******

The day of the get-together arrived. Leo set out with his fiddle, planning to be at Sandy Bell's before any of the others so he could get their drinks as they arrived. He was alone, Fiona would join him later, as he cut through to the Queensferry Road. Avoiding Princess Street, he continued onto Lothian Road and entered The Meadows at Melville Drive. It was a fine clear day, and the lush green grass and pinks and purples of the blossom lifted his spirits as he strolled along the tree-lined pathways. He left at George Square Lane which led to Forrest Road and Sandy Bell's.

When Leo walked in, Sean was already there, perched on a stool at the bar. He wasn't a regular in there, but he knew the bar staff alright and quickly ordered Leo a pint.

'So, all's well that ends well,' he said, as he passed Leo the glass.

'I hope so, cheers!'

'You're welcome, Joey will be along later with Jean and Andy.'

'Great, I'm looking forward to meeting Joey.'

Just then, Fergus, Sheedy, Pat and Mary came in complete with instruments. They'd booked in at the nearby Ibis Hotel for a couple of nights and had spent the morning sightseeing before having lunch. Leo introduced them to Sean and got them all a drink.

By the time Fiona had arrived, with Crina, Barsha and a couple more friends, the place was buzzing. The local musicians had started playing and seeing the visitors with instruments, had invited them to join in. Sean's sister, Claire and his two nieces plus a few friends of the family had all joined the party.

Sean introduced Leo and Fiona to Jim, the guy who had passed out at the Banshee and as Jim was relating his version of the story in an excitable and animated manner, Jean and Andy came in. Sean interrupted the conversation to introduce them.

'Leo, this is Jean and Andy, who you've met once before, and this is their son, Joey.'

Joey was wide eyed, 'I cannae believe it,' he said, as he hugged Leo and tears welled in his eyes.

'Joey,' Leo said, 'I didn't know Kevin so I don't know what he was like and I can't be him, but I'm going to look out for you as best I can. Shall I see if I can get some tickets for the football eh?'

'That'd be great.'

'Now, what are you all having to drink?' Leo offered.

The drinks were got, and the group were chatting when two uniformed police officers came in and approached them.

One of them spoke.

'We have a warrant for the arrest of Joseph Anderson, Mrs Anderson you can come with him.'

A worried Joey looked at his mother.

'It's alright Joey, let's go with them, see what they want,' she said and took his hand.

The room fell silent as they were led outside.

An awaiting police minibus took them to the station where they were led through reception to an office where a row of officers stood and applauded. Detective Inspector Barnhurst and Detective Superintendent Caldwell were stood at a desk. Caldwell spoke formally at first,

'Joseph Anderson, please accept this cheque and certificate as a token of our appreciation of the help you have given us.'

He then continued, 'Before we take you back to the party, we must issue you with a warning. Although in this instance you have been a great help to us, we must advise you to refrain from climbing into cemeteries or on to factory roofs in future, now off you go and enjoy the rest of your day.'

******

At a window table in Doctors pub, just down the street from Sandy Bell's, two old boys were sat with their drams and halves.

'I'd swear I saw Kevin Consadigne walk past here earlier, had his fiddle with him too,' says the one.'

'That can't be right, can it?' says the other.

The End

About the Author

Gerard Quinn was born in Wolverhampton to Irish parents. After a career of 32 years in engineering, he has spent the last 14 years working with disabled children and young adults. His interests include playing and listening to Scottish and Irish traditional music and travelling and walking in these two countries.

Thanks to:

Special Thanks to Bella James for the cover painting, Peter Hepworth for proofing and advice, Tim Vincent for technical assistance and to all the wonderful characters of Edinburgh who were the inspiration for this novel.

Printed in Great Britain
by Amazon